ICE

Books By Phyllis Reynolds Naylor

ICE

PHYLLIS REYNOLDS NAYLOR

A JEAN KARL BOOK

ATHENEUM
BOOKS FOR YOUNG READERS

Atheneum Books for Young Readers
An imprint of Simon & Schuster Children's Publishing Division
1230 Avenue of the Americas
New York, New York 10020

The text of this book is set in Bitstream Aldine 401
10   9   8   7   6   5   4
Printed in the United States of America
First edition

Library of Congress Cataloging-in-Publication Data

Naylor, Phyllis Reynolds.
Ice / Phyllis Reynolds Naylor. — 1st ed.
p. cm.
"A Jean Karl book."
Summary: When thirteen-year-old Chrissa is sent to her paternal
grandmother's farm, she learns more about her absent father and some of
the reasons for her distant relationship with her mother.
ISBN 0-689-80005-3
[1. Fathers and daughters—Fiction. 2. Mothers and daughters—Fiction.
3. Grandmothers—Fiction. 4. Family problems—Fiction.
5. Self-perception—Fiction. 6. Farm life—Fiction.] I. Title.
PZ7.N24Ic 1996
95-5279
[Fic]—dc20
CIP
AC

To three authors and friends, Joan Carris,
Marguerite Murray, and Peggy Thomson,
who richly deserve to have their names on this page,
and to my editor, Jean Karl, with gratitude

1

The earliest memory she had of her father was of going with him to the pier at Forty-second Street. They had driven over from Nineteenth in Chelsea—must have, because that's where she was born. He was taking her to see the Queen Elizabeth II.

Perhaps it was more his telling of it she remembered, but she recalled going up a steep ramp and walking in close quarters down hallways. She and her father had peered into rooms where there were large bouquets and laughing people.

This much she was sure she remembered: "Someday I'm going to live by the water," he had told her. And at four or five, she had believed whatever he said.

◆ ◆ ◆

"Chrissa," her mother told her at breakfast, "we're not going to go on like this—those looks you give me, your silences . . . It's wearing us both down."

There was that tugging feeling in her throat again. Chrissa pressed her spoon flat into the grapefruit and watched it fill with juice. Say something! she told herself, but the words hung frozen, like icicles, inside her. Loneliness, hurt, and anger, one heaped on top the other, kept

1

her silent. The girl with the layered look.

It was Mother who should have been doing the talking, anyway—who should have explained what had happened between her and Dad three years ago, and where Chrissa's father had gone. But all this seemed to be frozen inside Mom as well.

Now Mom's eyes were watching hers, blue like her own. "For the last year, you've been impossible," Mother continued. "Once you started junior high, you just clammed up. Do you know what it's like to come home from work each day to someone who won't even talk to you?"

Again the pause. The spoon filled with juice, and Chrissa swallowed mechanically. She really did wish she could think of something, but the words would be spiteful.

"I'm sending you to live with Gram for a year. We need a rest from each other."

No! Chrissa loosened her grip on the spoon and stared at her mother. She must be joking.

"I've checked the train schedule. You'll be leaving the day after classes are out next month, and will start school there in the fall." Mother was studying her intently. Her eyes were anxious. Loving, even.

"Y-you don't have to do this." Chrissa's words came out weak, raspy. It was all she could manage; no promises, no apologies.

"Do you have a better idea? I can only see things getting worse between us, and you won't talk to the counselor at school. Someone has to do something, and Gram said she'd try."

Mom didn't understand. The counselor was there only on Thursday mornings, and you had to sign up three weeks in advance. Besides, if Chrissa couldn't talk to her mother, how could she talk to someone she didn't even know?

And so when school was out Chrissa, still disbelieving, found herself standing wordlessly at the gate in Penn Station. Any minute Mom would say, "Oh, why don't you stay? We'll give it one more try." But she didn't.

What she said was "Honey, try to look at this as an adventure, okay?" Her eyes were wet.

The attendant removed the rope at the escalator, and the crowd surged forward. With her vinyl bag bumping against one leg, another bag over her shoulder, Chrissa moved away from her mother's embrace.

"Chrissa's Great Adventure," she said to herself. "She sees the escalator, she approaches the escalator, and . . ." Chrissa put one foot on the moving stairs. *"Takeoff!"*

She didn't look back.

As the train rolled away from the station, Chrissa was astonished to discover she was fighting back tears. She turned them into angry tears, and that helped. She felt better when she was angry. When you were angry, you did things to other people. When you were sad, you let them do things to you. What kind of mother would send her own daughter away? It only made the feelings worse.

"Are you all right?" The woman on the seat beside her had noticed.

"Yes."

"Like a tissue?"

Chrissa took it wordlessly, cheeks burning. She hadn't thought to bring Kleenex; hadn't known she was going to cry.

"Is there anything I can do?"

Chrissa shook her head and turned toward the window. *Leave me alone*, she wanted to say. That was one of the troubles. There were only women in her life—no father, no grandfather, no uncles, no boyfriend . . .

She sighed and thought of what lay ahead. She felt at home with sidewalks and steps, the bus stops and stores of New York City, but had never much liked the small house where her grandmother lived outside Rochester, surrounded by a yard that would be a whole city block back home.

She had enjoyed the yard when she was younger, but she did not like the nothingness—no music, no streetlights, no cars or crowds. Gram herself was far older, it seemed, than anyone else's grandmother, sneaking a cigarette in the bathroom but telling everyone she didn't smoke. *Yeah, send me to Gram's. Great role model, Mom.*

There were not, of course, many relatives to take her in. Gramps was dead, and on Mom's side of the family, her mother was in a nursing home in California, and her father had died in a drunken stupor. Maybe this was why Mom had remained friendly with her mother-in-law after Dad left—there weren't numerous caring relatives for her, either.

Chrissa decided one thing, however; somehow, someway, she would find out from Gram what had happened to Dad. About that she was determined. Maybe this would be a bigger adventure than Mom had bargained for. Chrissa Jennings, girl detective, on her way to meet her white-haired contact.

The really weird part was that she couldn't remember exactly what her father looked like, the enigmatic stranger who entered her life at intervals. The most recent picture

4

she had of him was taken years ago at Coney Island, when Chrissa was six. His mustache was dark, to match his hair, and his eyes a deep brown. When she had last seen him, at ten, what did he look like then?

He could have changed a lot in three years. Would she recognize him if she saw him on the street? If he were on this train, even? She glanced around. Some businessmen across the aisle, and the portly conductor; that was all.

"Tickets, please. All tickets."

Chrissa opened her bag.

◆ ◆ ◆

She held back as the row of two-seater cars clanked noisily over the last rise and rolled to a stop in front of her. He gave her hand a little jerk.

"C'mon. I've got tickets for three rides."

"No . . ."

"I'll be right beside you!"

She shook her head.

"Will you try it if I go first?"

Chrissa did not answer as her father stepped into one of the little cars on the Cyclone and sat with his knees scrunched up, pulling the bar down across his lap. He had bribed the attendant to admit Chrissa, but still she refused.

She realized she would soon be the only one left on the platform, and her chest tightened with indecision as she looked at the empty space beside her father.

He grinned at her as the cars lurched forward suddenly, bumping into each other, and then, with a steady grinding sound, began their slow climb.

Loneliness welled inside her as the car with her father in it moved away. She could feel the vibration of his leave-taking

5

through the soles of her shoes, and for years afterward the longing for him began first as a tingling in the bottom of her feet before it reached her heart.

She stood there beside a short, wiry man with a tattoo on each arm, who waited with his hand on a lever, cigarette dangling from his lips. Her eyes followed the lights strung along the entire length of the roller coaster, over every hill and down again, around and under.

When the Cyclone rolled into the station at last, her father was still smiling. "C'mon! You'll like it!"

She shook her head.

Chrissa's father got out of the car. She smiled up at him as he took her hand to guide her through the crowd.

"Wouldn't have hurt you at all to try," he said. "Show a little spunk now and then."

It was all she remembered of Coney Island. That and the fact that one moment he was smiling and the next he was not.

◆ ◆ ◆

When Chrissa got off the train, her contact was waiting, purse tucked under one arm. Gram's stockingless feet were thrust into Dr. Scholl's sandals, her gray hair cut in a no-nonsense bob. She was somewhere in her seventies, Chrissa knew. *Agent X76.* Would she come through?

Gram gave no outward show of affection, for which Chrissa was grateful. Simply latched onto Chrissa's arm and gave it a little squeeze.

"Lorraine says she's shipping the rest of your things next week, so we'll drive right home, huh?"

"Okay."

"You hungry? Get anything to eat on the train?"

"I'm fine."

Gram's car was an ancient green Plymouth with ripped

seats, and she had to try twice to start it. Out on the road, she hardly seemed tall enough to see over the steering wheel. Chrissa watched uncertainly. When cars passed on the left, she wasn't sure Gram saw them at all. In fact, Gram went straight through a red light and didn't notice.

Dear Mom, This is a great adventure. I'm so glad you suggested it. I doubt that either Gram or I will make it home alive.

2

Within ten minutes of leaving the train station, they were in country. The hills were low, rolling, covered with green, and the air had a primitive smell, dank and pungent—wet earth and fertilizer, rotting wood, warm cattle.

"I was trying to remember when you were here last, Chrissie," Gram said. "You were eleven, I think."

"Ten. Just before Dad . . . left." There. She had given the password, but Agent X76 was cagey.

"I have the pond then?"

"No."

"Neighbor put it in for me. Always wanted a pond. The goldfish don't last too long, though, with raccoons around, but I just buy me some more."

Gram drove with her head high, as though hoisted by invisible string. Her bright red lipstick bled into tiny lines about her lips, giving them a frayed look like old curtains, and her hands had developed large brown freckles on the backs, something Chrissa had not noticed before.

Chrissa studied the landscape again. Where did people shop for clothes out here? See a movie? Get their hair cut? What kept them from bursting out of their houses and going nuts under this wide and silent sky?

She reached out and turned the knob on the radio, but nothing happened.

"Broke," said Gram. "Played for one month after I bought the car, and hasn't played since."

Chrissa closed her eyes.

"I asked the school for their summer reading list, and got you some books. Not too much for a girl to do out here, but we'll find some places to go, you and me."

Thirty minutes out of Rochester, Gram turned up the long gravel drive to her house. It looked even older than Chrissa remembered, paint peeling from its door and window frames. A wooden hen and chicks marched across the front lawn, and up near the bushes stood a plaster doe and fawn.

Tacky, Chrissa thought, even though she remembered petting them when she was younger.

"Well, here we are!" Gram said.

Dutifully Chrissa climbed out, took her other bag from the backseat, and followed her grandmother to the door.

The house smelled—first thing Chrissa noticed. Smelled of old books and fabric, mildew and bacon grease.

Something bumped against her leg and she startled.

Gram laughed. "Only Shadow," she said, as a gray cat with white paws turned around in front of Chrissa and came back, rubbing the other side of its body against her leg.

A yellow cat appeared from under the table.

"Bess," said Gram, by way of introduction. "Guess you wouldn't remember them, would you? They both wandered in here the last year or two."

Chrissa winced. There had never been pets in their apartment in New York City. Making a wide half-circle around the yellow cat, she walked on into the parlor, idly picking up the glass paperweight that snowed when you shook it. She touched a pink shell on the table. The things she remembered from childhood, however, had no hold on her now.

The steps to the second floor dipped in the middle from foot traffic over the years. There were three bedrooms at the top, just as Chrissa remembered. One was Gram's, every inch taken up with knickknacks and plastic flowers. The second contained pure junk—a storeroom for the unwanted. The third bedroom, and smallest, would be hers.

Chrissa sucked in her breath.

It looked like a guest room for bag ladies—a hideous orange chenille spread on the bed; floral curtains yellowed with age; a linoleum floor with braided rugs scattered here and there. One scratched bureau; dresser with monstrous round mirror that Chrissa remembered; and a bookcase filled with *Reader's Digest*s. This room smelled too—dust and floor wax and stored-away clothes at the back of the closet.

Dear Mother, I think there has been a mistake. I have ended up in a used-furniture store among the rejects.

"You can move whatever you don't want to the spare bedroom," Gram told her. "I'll start dinner, and let you put your things away wherever you like."

Chrissa stood in the center of the room, staring in dismay at the faded pictures on the walls—a dark vase with dark flowers; a couple gazing out over a lake. The two cats sat at a distance in the hall, studying the new arrival.

Sitting down heavily on the bed, Chrissa felt tears spring to her eyes again. She was trapped in a room she could not stand another minute! Silently she wiped two fingers across her eyes. How had she let this happen?

"Talk to me!" Mother had yelled once outside her door. Yelled so loud that Chrissa knew the Westfalls could probably hear her in the apartment below. "You can be just as hostile by clamming up, you know."

But Chrissa hadn't opened her door. A coward, that's what she was. Maybe she was afraid that if she started talking, she wouldn't be able to stop. And perhaps, if she couldn't stop talking, she couldn't stop crying, either.

She spread her hands out on the bed behind her, and her fingers touched a small sheet of notepaper near the pillow.

Chrissa, it said at the top. She picked it up:

This is my house, so I make the rules:
1. *You always tell me where you're going.*
2. *You return when I say.*
3. *No friends in unless I'm here.*
4. *All homework done before watching TV.*
5. *Three meals a week to be cooked by you; also half the housework.*
6. *No lies.*

Indignation swept over her, and she gave a bitter laugh. Friends? *What* friends? And where would she go?

The yellow cat came walking pointedly across the braided rug, sniffed at her bag for a moment, then tensed its hind legs and jumped on the bed.

Chrissa scooted quickly away. "Get off! Shoo!"

The cat paused. She was a large cat, fat as a throw pillow, and began making pawing motions, bedding down.

"Go! I don't want your fleas!" Chrissa leaped up, grabbing hold of the spread, and gave it a hard shake.

The cat held on, ears laid back, until the shaking subsided, then lay down and yawned.

◆ ◆ ◆

Sometimes, when Dad came home, Mother put on new shoes or a different color of lipstick. "It's fun to surprise him," she said.

Chrissa decided to surprise him too. She hid in the cupboard under the sink, and heard the click of the door as her father entered the apartment, Mother's squeal, the "Hi, babe!" and the usual rustle of packages.

"Chrissa in bed?"

"No, she's been waiting for you. Chrissa!" called Mother.

Chrissa's heart pounded with excitement.

Mother called again. "Daddy's here!" There was the sound of her footsteps coming toward the kitchen. She flicked on the light. Chrissa could see the sliver of yellow in the crack between the cupboard doors. "Where the heck could she be? She was just here!"

"Well, I guess she doesn't want this big old present I bought for her, then. I'll go down and give it to that little raggedy kid I saw on the corner."

He wouldn't!

"It's such a big, cuddly bear," said Mother.

They were teasing. She'd make them come and find her. But then she heard her father's footsteps in the hallway, the click of the door as it opened.

She sprang out of the cupboard, banging her knee, scrambling through the kitchen and into the next room just as the front door closed.

"Daddy!" she screamed, but it was too late.

She threw herself on the couch and sobbed, and suddenly the

12

door opened again. Her father came in sober-faced.

"Little kid on the corner sure did like that bear," said Nick.

Chrissa cried all the harder. And then, before he closed the door, her father reached outside and pulled in after him the largest teddy bear Chrissa had ever seen. Her shoulders shook as one last sob escaped her; then she ran across the room and threw her arms around the bear.

Her father laughed. "Won't try that again, will you, kiddo?"

He was lifting her up, high in the air, and she was shrieking. Chrissa laughed and her father laughed and Mom was laughing too. Suddenly it was laughing time in the apartment on Nineteenth Street.

3

Next order of business: reconnoiter. Spies had been trapped in conditions far worse than these.

"I'm going outside, it's cooler," she said to Gram.

Chrissa stood on the back porch in the late afternoon sun and expelled all the air in her lungs to get rid of the stale tobacco smell and mildew, then drank in the scent of trees and grass.

In New York City, on her block, the trees had scrawny trunks. Up here, however, they were massive, trunks separating into limbs higher up, then branches that disappeared into leafiness so thick and dark that not a trace of sunlight filtered through.

There was a two-seater swing at one end of the pond. The pond itself, as big as a dining table, as round as the moon, had been scooped out of the middle of the yard, the rim of its prefab liner showing around the top. Chrissa liked the lily pads floating on the surface, however.

She walked across the grass and sank down in the swing under the willow. This was where she was going to stay as much as possible until the year was up. In sun and rain and snow she'd sit here, out of that smelly house.

Some small thing jumped on the water's surface, and Chrissa leaned forward. Water bug? It was a strange insect, with wire-thin legs that skimmed the pond in swift, jerky thrusts. Chrissa settled down again and, like an insect herself, quickly pushed her feet against the ground, back and forth, back and forth.

◆ ◆ ◆

"He said he'd buy me a goldfish."

Chrissa stood at the door of her parents' bedroom, and had to repeat it twice before Mother put down her magazine.

"Well, it doesn't look like he's going to, so forget it."

"Dad SAID!"

"For heaven's sake, Chrissa, I'LL buy you a goldfish. How many do you want?

"I want HIM to buy one for me."

"God almighty, will you stop being so difficult?"

◆ ◆ ◆

The screen slammed and Gram came across the lawn, wiping her hands on a dish towel. "Well, now, how do you like my pond?"

Chrissa was so used to not answering that she had to force the words out. "Better than my room," she said.

The rudeness of her remark hung in the air like a flag. Major blunder. Establish trust with X76. Perhaps Gram hadn't noticed, however, because she sat down on the swing beside Chrissa, forcing her to scoot over. Then she gave a contented sigh. "Oh, I do like this pond. Water never looks the same twice. Probably because the sky is different. Isn't exactly beachfront property, but the pond's as close as I'll get, I imagine."

15

This was Chrissa's cue: "Dad always wanted to live by the ocean, didn't he?"

At first she felt that Agent X76 was not going to answer. But finally Gram said, "Nick likes the sea as well as anybody, I imagine. Always liked swimming when he was a boy."

"Does he live near the ocean now?"

"Near enough."

"Does he ever visit you?"

"I get a letter now and then."

"Well, I'd like to write to him," Chrissa said. "Could I have his address?"

This time she felt sure Agent X76 was toying with her, Gram waited so long to reply. Finally the old woman said, "I guess you'd have to get that from your mom, Chrissie."

"Why?"

"Because if Lorraine had wanted you writing him, she would have given you his address herself."

"But you're his mother!"

"That's my only claim. He's Lorraine's ex-husband and the father of her child. You'll have to ask her."

"Mom and I haven't been talking much."

"So I've heard." Two minutes went by, then three, with only the creak of the swing doing the talking. Then Gram said, "I think I like it better out here myself, Chrissie."

Dinner was awful. Greasy fried potatoes, stewed meat, canned green beans, and stale biscuits served cold. The only really edible thing on the table was strawberries, which Gram had picked fresh.

"No appetite?" Gram studied her from across the table.

Chrissa shook her head. *Not for this*, she wanted to say, but didn't. She helped herself to more strawberries.

"What I always wanted," Gram said, continuing the conversation they had begun in the yard, "is not what I got, but near enough, I figure. Always wanted fruit trees in my backyard and the ocean out front. Got a pond and a strawberry patch, so I can't complain."

She sent Chrissa back upstairs after dinner to finish her unpacking. Chrissa braced herself for the task of stowing her clothes in the sour-smelling drawers of the old dresser. She traded her gauze blouse for a T-shirt, pinned her long brown hair up off the nape of her neck, then pulled out each drawer and turned it upside down over the wastebasket to rid it of dead moths, bits of paper, and the lint of all the lives that had passed through this upstairs room.

When she finished, she sorted idly through the stack of library books Gram had left on top of her dresser with the eighth-grade summer reading list—*Shabanu, A Separate Peace, To Kill a Mockingbird, Send No Blessings* . . . Chrissa sprawled out on the bed and looked through the low windows on the other side. Trees, trees, and—beyond the trees—hills spreading out to even more trees farther on.

She rolled over on her back, staring up at the ceiling, one gray cobweb strung between picture frame and light. A tear leaked out the corner of her eye and lost itself in her ear. How had she got from the little kid who used to pet Gram's plastic deer to the unhappy person she was now?

It was all Mom's fault. Or, if he was alive, Dad's. But a third possibility flickered in her mind: her very own fault, for failing to be the kind of daughter a dad would want to be around.

◆ ◆ ◆

He parked just outside the drugstore, where there was no meter, engine running.

17

"If a policeman comes by," Chrissa's father told her, "tell him your daddy will be right out; he went to get you some medicine."

"I'm not sick!" she protested.

"I went to get some medicine for you, understand?"

It seemed he was gone forever. Any minute Chrissa expected the police to come and take the car away. It began to shudder, and then the engine died completely. When her father came back, there were tears running down Chrissa's face.

"Oh, for Pete's sake," he said, whether about her or the engine, she wasn't sure. He slid in and placed a carton of cigarettes on the seat beside him. As he started the car again and pulled away from the curb with a squeal of tires, he said, "You're one sorry pup, you know it?"

◆ ◆ ◆

"Well! You made quick work of that!"

She was still lying on the bed when Gram came up for inspection. "Looks good!" she said. "Now, if it gets too warm up here, there's a fan at the back of your closet."

Chrissa gave no answer. When a minute had passed she rolled moodily over on her stomach again without a word.

Gram went to the window and sat down on a trunk. "The only way this is going to work, Chrissa-girl," she said, "is if we talk to each other. It can be angry talk, sad talk, any sort at all, but it's better than keeping it locked up." She waited some more. "What I like to do is take a glass of iced tea and go sit on the swing till dark. Want some?"

Still Chrissa did not respond. Her face, she knew, was as smooth and cold as a slab of stone, but on the inside she felt small and pitiful, torn into a thousand pieces.

"Well," said her grandmother finally, getting up. "You can come or not." And she went downstairs.

She didn't really mean Chrissa could talk about anything at all; what she meant was "anything at all besides your father," Chrissa decided.

"Is he dead? Just tell me that," Chrissa had demanded once when she saw her mother packing up his clothes, along with all the things in his drawers, to send to Gram.

"For heaven's sake, Chrissa, we've separated and are going to divorce. Can't we leave it at that?"

"Then why doesn't he come for his things?"

"Nick has always had enough money to buy whatever he wants. He can easily start again. We're just not a part of his life anymore, and it's easier on all of us to forget him. I know that sounds hard, Chrissa, but trust me."

Forget him? Chrissa had thought. Forget Nick Jennings, the wavy-haired mystery man who came home laden with gifts, then was off again for weeks, sometimes a month at a time? He was a salesman of some sort. Auto parts, Mother said.

"Is that your *father*?" Chrissa's girlfriends used to ask as he sat out on the steps of the apartment building, smoking a cigarette, the crease in his pants as clean and fine as a paper edge, smiling his wonderful smile.

How would Chrissa *know* he wasn't dead unless she could see him again or hear his voice? If you were divorcing your husband and he didn't come back for his things, wouldn't you just throw them out? Why, unless he was dead, would you pack everything up and send them to his mother?

Now Chrissa got up and opened a drawer, taking out the cap Dad sometimes wore when they went out together—a Greek fisherman's cap, set at a jaunty angle on his head. She had rescued it from his closet when Mom wasn't look-

19

ing and kept it all this time. She traced the dark blue braid above the bill with one finger, holding it close to her face, and drank in the familiar scent of his hair.

When Gram came in at last, Chrissa went out. She made her way across the grass toward the white wooden swing that beckoned to her in the dusk.

Something darted in front of her and Chrissa froze, heart thumping, then saw that it was Shadow, almost invisible in the dark. She reached the swing and sat down. The night seemed alive with noise. Listening attentively, Chrissa could tell that there were several sounds, not just one—a mixed chorus of she didn't know how many voices. Every so often there would be a screech from the trees, then a trill from the bushes, followed by indescribable sounds from the pond. What *was* all this?

She shivered slightly and turned to look over her shoulder, then jerked her head back again. Her eye caught something tall and thick, gray as day-old snow in the city, mottled with patches of brown and yellow. In the near dark, the sycamore's bark stood out from the rest, having the appearance of a horse's dappled coat, sleek and smooth.

Chrissa didn't know why, but she liked seeing it there— liked knowing that through all the changes that had happened to her and Mom and Gram, it stood its ground, steady and strong. There used to be a rubber tire hanging from it when she was five, when Gramps was alive. The swing was gone, but the sycamore remained. Maybe she was crazy, but the first friend she was making up here was this tree.

4

It was an uneasy night. Things were just too strange. Chrissa was conscious of a faint dusty smell, and the scent of sheets that had been stored too long in a closet. Weird sounds came from beyond the screens—a hoot, a trill, a squawk, a croak. Noises that might have seemed normal in the light of day were grotesque sounding in the dark.

She got up once for a drink of water and found what she was sure was the world's largest roach in the bathtub. She fled back to her room. *Dear Mom, Are you out of your mind? This is a jungle! I want to come home!*

At some point there was a noise close by, and Chrissa went to the window, resting her hands on the sill. All she saw was the sycamore. It seemed to have moved closer to the house, as though trees and bushes changed places under cover of darkness and were crowding in, surrounding her.

At breakfast she found Gram frying eggs, with a tea towel pinned to the front of her sheer navy dress. There was the stub of a cigarette in a saucer on the counter, and Chrissa was tempted to comment. What she said was "Looks like you're going somewhere," and sat down at the table in the long T-shirt she slept in.

"Sunday service," said Gram. "You want your eggs fried or scrambled?"

"Fried will do." Chrissa reached for the lone slice of toast. She was surprised to discover that she felt somewhat better. Things looked a bit more hopeful in daylight.

Gram slipped the eggs onto a plate. "Come along if you want. Dress any way you like, long as it's decent."

"Okay, I'll come." Chrissa could tell by Gram's expression that she was pleased. What she didn't know was that Chrissa would prefer being almost anywhere other than this smelly house. "What church is it?"

"Sister Harmony's Whole Body Church of the Lord is what it is, except it meets outside in a tent."

Good Grief. "Protestant, or what?"

Gram stood in front of the small mirror above the sink, unpinned the tea towel, and straightened the collar of her dress. "Well, now, I don't know that it's anything you can put a label on. What's important to Sister Harmony is that your body, mind, and spirit are all working together."

"Whatever," said Chrissa, and finished her toast. Then, "The world's largest cockroach was in our tub last night."

Gram broke into sudden laughter. "That was just an old wood roach, Chrissie! You'll see those now and then in the country. I saw it too before I went to bed. It was still there this morning, so I took it outside in a cup."

Chrissa reddened, but managed a smile.

"How did you sleep?"

"Okay, I guess. Lot of noise out there."

"Oh, Chrissie, wait till spring when the peepers are out. There's a little bog over in my woods, and you get a whole chorus of peepers going, sounds like sleigh bells."

"What *are* they?"

22

"Tree frogs. Tiny little reddish-brown things. Hard to spot, though. Went out one night with my boots and flashlight, determined I was going to see one. Soon's I got to the bog, of course, they all stopped peeping. Had to stand in that water ten minutes before they began again. You remind me, we'll go next spring."

"I'll pass," Chrissa told her. *Dear Mom, My dream come true: I've been invited to go wading in a bog.*

For Sunday service, Chrissa put on the same gauze blouse she'd worn the day before, and fastened her hair up off her neck. Then she got in the old Plymouth, the sun already baking the vinyl seats, and closed her eyes. They popped open again as the car lurched forward, turned around on the grass, and headed down the driveway.

"Why didn't you just back out?" Chrissa asked.

"Can't see. Knocked over my mailbox last time I tried that," said Gram. And with her neck stretched to the limit, she headed the car down the road.

"Are there any people my age up here?" Chrissa asked.

"I don't know that there are many girls, Chrissie. Come to think of it, I don't know a single family with girls."

Chrissa smiled at Gram. "Well, boys are people too."

Gram stared straight ahead.

"Are there any *boys*?" Chrissa asked directly.

"There's some."

"Where?"

"Chrissie, don't hurry your life along. You'll meet them in good time, I'll wager."

Chrissa plopped back against the seat and prepared to be bored.

The meeting of Sister Harmony's Whole Body Church of

the Lord was in somebody's side yard. In the open tent, about sixty folding chairs had been set up, fewer than half of them filled.

Sister Harmony stood in front, an imposing figure all in white, with gray hair, grayer than Gram's, that clung tightly to her head in waves. Her ankles and wrists were thick, and when she spread out her arms, the flesh quivered.

". . . all *three!*" she was saying. "All *three* work together to glorify our Lord. You can't heal the body if the mind is sick; can't heal the mind if the spirit is weak. God, who made us, can heal us."

The evangelist's eyes traveled over the small congregation. "But the Lord needs a token of your faith, my friends. You have to give generously *for* God to receive generously *from* God. If we find favor in His sight, we have a place reserved for us in the heavenly kingdom."

"Amen," said Gram.

Chrissa stole a look around her. Women. Mostly women. *The story of her life.* Women in flowered dresses who fanned themselves with the hymn sheets, watching the large polar bear of a woman up front. Chrissa smiled at the comparison, but it was the wrong time to smile. Sister Harmony saw.

"Sister Harmony knows," the big woman said, looking intently at Chrissa, and then on around the tent. "I know what's in your heart, because I see it on your face. The spirit feeds the mind and the mind shapes the face. It shows. Oh, let me tell you, it shows. . . ."

Chrissa looked uneasily away. Sister Harmony was talking now about the importance of honoring parents, and Chrissa realized it was Father's Day. She set herself the task of counting the men in the audience. Three: a man who

24

was half asleep; another with moonlike face; and a man with slick-backed hair and sideburns, sitting off to one side with a portable keyboard on his lap, waiting, it seemed, for a signal from Sister Harmony that he should play.

". . . Reservations for heaven must be made in advance, though. There's no box office at heaven's gate. When you give to God, He knows if it's all you can afford. God loves a cheerful giver, for you're investing in your future life."

Dear Mother, Chrissa began in her head. *You can't guess where I am now. . . .*

The longer she sat, the harder the seat, the warmer the air, the stickier her skirt against the backs of her thighs. Where was her own father, she wondered, on Father's Day?

◆ ◆ ◆

It was a hot night in New York City. Like soldiers crawling out of their trenches after the fighting was done, New Yorkers poked their heads from doorways testing the breeze, and finally ventured out to sit on the steps of brownstones or the black metal grids of fire escapes.

Chrissa took Piglet and her doll out on the steps with a blanket and told them a bedtime story.

Nick Jennings was all dressed up that night, sitting on the railing. Chrissa enjoyed the scent of his after-shave, and the way he wore a freshly laundered shirt, sleeves rolled up to the elbows, while other men sat around in undershirts. He was smoking a cigarette, and flicked the ashes on the stoop.

The doll closed her eyes immediately, of course, but Piglet took his time. Chrissa had to rock him awhile, making up songs about the day's adventures. Mr. and Mrs. Mulligan smiled at her from the neighboring stoop, but when she glanced up once at her father, he was looking beyond her with such impatience that she stopped singing in mid-verse and put Piglet right to bed.

25

A car pulled up and Nick slid off the railing.

"G'night, kid," he said, and walked to the car. Hoisting up one trouser leg slightly at the knee, he got in and the car drove off. He never heard the rest of her song.

If the Mulligans liked her, why couldn't he?

◆ ◆ ◆

Chrissa must not have been listening because she suddenly noticed that Sister Harmony's eyes were closed, her arms folded in an X over her chest as she rocked from side to side. The man with the keyboard began to play softly.

". . . and there's someone, Lord, with a bad back. There is a woman here—Lord, I can almost see who it is—whose knees hurt her so bad she can hardly walk up the stairs."

A gasp came from three or four women at once, Gram included. Requests for healing were being called out now—for a husband who drank too much, someone with a thyroid problem, foot troubles, high blood pressure . . . And then Chrissa was startled to hear Sister Harmony say:

"And there is a special request, Lord, for a person who comes here today with a different kind of hurt—the kind of hurt, Lord, that makes you want to hurt someone else. We come to you, Lord, with these hurt bodies, these hurt minds and spirits, and we know that you won't heal one till you can heal them all—that all three work together."

Gram's been talking to her, I'll bet! thought Chrissa.

She stared at the woman in white with the closed eyes, but didn't believe they were closed at all. Through those dark little slits she believed that Sister Harmony was watching her all the while. They reminded her uncomfortably of her father's eyes, the way he squinted sometimes

26

when he smoked. Chrissa never knew if he could see her then or not.

Afterward, as people left the tent, Gram shook hands with the preacher, but Chrissa hung back.

"Felt it was me you were praying over when you talked about those knees," Gram told Sister Harmony.

"He knows what you need before you ask it," the woman replied. Before Sister Harmony could turn to her, however, Chrissa slipped around the couple in front of them and made her escape. She had never felt so uneasy as she had in the tent, nor so relieved to step outside.

The sultry closeness of the air made nothing seem worth doing. Gram had fixed grilled cheese sandwiches for lunch, and they sat limply on each plate with a spoonful of canned applesauce to one side.

"It's too hot to eat anything warm," Chrissa said miserably.

Gram chewed with enthusiasm. "There's tuna in the cupboard, you want that," she offered.

Chrissa pushed away from the table, hot and exasperated. She sat with her arms dangling, staring out a side window. The spy motif had already played itself out.

"I'm hot, I'm miserable, and I don't like Sister Harmony," she said suddenly. There! She was talking, wasn't she?

Her grandmother observed her quietly for a moment. "Chrissie, it's like you're soured on life."

It was too much. Tears sprang to Chrissa's eyes. "It's not me, it's *here*! This place! Everything's old. It smells! And I miss my dad!"

Lord, now she'd done it. Surprisingly, however, Gram

didn't seem too upset. She took another bite of applesauce, studying Chrissa all the while:

"You can change where you live, Chrissie, and the clothes you put on your back, but until you change what's wrong inside you, you'll feel the same as before."

"*What's* wrong inside me? What are you talking about?"

Gram didn't take her eyes away. "You've got a long list of things you hate, Chrissie. What do you love?"

"What *is* there to love?" Chrissa demanded rudely.

And Gram answered, "Yourself."

The answer had been so unexpected that after a few minutes more of glaring out the window, Chrissa got up and went outside to cool off. Even the yard was hot, however, so she set out for the woods beyond.

The more she thought about Gram's remark, the more surprised she was. That she didn't love her mother enough or Gram enough or the world in general, she could understand. But herself?

Her legs were too skinny, too much like Gram's. Her shoulders were narrow, her waist too thick, and those were only her physical defects.

Kindness? Fifty percent. Intelligence? Probably more than she displayed at school. Courage? Ten percent. She would never be the spunky adventurous girl her father would have liked her to be. Too much like Mom, a city girl through and through. Dad had wanted her carved in his own image, yet when was he ever home to help?

The first two years after he left—"disappeared," was the way Chrissa thought of it—she was too hurt, too numb, to feel anger. How could you be angry at the person you longed to have back? But why had he not said

28

good-bye? Why hadn't he written or called?

Chrissa had gone only twenty feet or so into the woods when she realized she was surrounded entirely by trees. She had never, strangely, ventured into Gram's woods at all when she'd visited here before, content to play on the grass and in the large tub of water Gram used to provide.

She stood still and listened. All she could hear was the thrubbing of her pulse in her temples.

There was a log farther on, one end resting upon the stump from which it had fallen. She would go as far as that, she decided, and when she got there, felt quite proud of herself to be sitting alone in the woods, not scared half out of her mind. She felt, in fact, a part of the woods, still and mysterious. Could she keep this little bit of quiet with her, enough to get along with Gram for a year? She took a deep breath of the air around her. She could *smell* the calm. It smelled of bark and damp.

If her father *was* alive, might he come by sometime to see her? He'd just be taking a little walk, maybe, and here was this girl, bold as brass, sitting off in the woods, not a bit scared. He might not even recognize her.

5

It was obvious that if there were other people around, Chrissa was going to have to discover them herself.

She went back to the house finally and into the dining room. Gram was sitting beside a sewing basket at the table.

"I'd like to find a job," Chrissa told her.

Gram was trying to thread a needle. She held it out in front of her and made a quick jab with the thread. Missed.

"What kind of job did you have in mind?"

"Anyone you know needing a sitter? I've been taking care of the little boy below us in Chelsea. I was his favorite sitter."

"Way out here, it would be mostly day jobs, Chrissie—a full-time sitter. Wouldn't be much point driving you clear into Rochester to sit a couple of hours for people who want to see a movie."

"Any stores hiring, then? McDonald's or something?"

"Aren't many of those kinds of jobs around here either. This far out, it's farms, mostly. You can check the *Democrat Chronicle,* but I doubt it."

"Well, what kind of work *is* there, then?"

"Mainly the kind I do. Old woman needs someone three mornings a week—wash her hair, cook her meals. I take care of a newborn baby twice a week—that kind of thing."

"But if you hear of somebody needing a sitter evenings, will you recommend me?"

Gram put the needle down momentarily, still unthreaded. "Well, now, Chrissie, I can tell them all about how you were at seven or ten, but I don't know a thing about the kind of worker you are at thirteen."

Chrissa felt hopeless. "Well, it's sort of impossible then, isn't it?"

"Depends," said Gram, and, picking up the needle, took another jab.

Chrissa sat down in the straight-backed chair across from her. "Okay, what do I have to do?"

Gram smiled. "Well, half the housework, for one. And you need to think about the meals you'll be making here. I shop on Mondays, so I'll need your grocery list by then."

This was going to be one tough old lady.

"What should I cook?"

"Whatever you like. What do you eat at home?"

"Stouffers, mainly."

"Stouffers isn't going to get any of my money just for putting food in plastic bags. There're cookbooks in the kitchen. Figure something out."

Chrissa took a deep breath. "Let me thread that needle for you," she said.

She spent the rest of the afternoon on a rusty folding chair in the shade of the sycamore, with a cookbook from the Cooperative Farm Women of Monroe County on her lap. After making it through the beef section, she leaned her head back, hands trailing in the grass.

Chrissa noticed that the sycamore's leaves were huge, very different from the rest of the trees around it. She knew none of the others by name, but turning her head slowly, she studied their leaves. Some leaves were slim and pointed, like an arrowhead; some were eight or ten to a stem, like a fern. But the sycamore's leaves were largest of all—broad as a man's hand. She wondered about her father's hands. How could she not remember?

◆ ◆ ◆

She was walking down the street beside him the day after her sixth birthday. Her hand was in his, and from time to time she pulled it close to her face to enjoy his scent—a metallic smell from his car keys; a tobacco smell. A smell of leather car upholstery; of sweat.

She looked up suddenly to see a man with a dog coming toward them. A large dog with eyes like the black buttons on her coat. Its mouth was open, dripping saliva, and when it saw Chrissa, it tensed, straining at the leash until its whole body leaned sideways.

She clung to her father, fingers gripping the cloth of his trousers. The dog came closer still, and she screamed, trying to squeeze between her father's legs.

And then his voice: "For God's sake, Chrissa. Don't be such a baby."

◆ ◆ ◆

"How about tuna casserole, hamburgers, and spaghetti?" she asked Gram later when she went inside.

"Sounds fine to me. Be sure to make a vegetable."

At dinner that evening, a better meal because Gram had baked chicken, a question about Chrissa's father came up naturally. Asked which she preferred, white meat or dark, Chrissa answered, "Dark," and Gram smiled a bit.

"Same with Nick," she murmured.

"What else did he like?" Chrissa asked pleasantly.

32

"Well, now, you surely could answer that yourself."

"Even when he lived with us, he was gone a lot." Chrissa strung out the conversation like a fisherman letting out line. "He used to bring home a pizza once in a while. He liked that. What would you cook if he came to visit?"

Gram picked up her knife and sliced methodically at the meat on her plate. "Well, it's been a while."

"Does he know I'm here?" Chrissa couldn't resist.

"He knows."

Chrissa studied her grandmother carefully. "Think he might come by to see me?"

She was surprised at Gram's reply: "I doubt it. You just have to get thoughts like that out of your head."

Disappointment careened through Chrissa's body. "But why?" She already suspected.

"Oh, Chrissie, how do *I* know a man's mind? If he hasn't been to see you the last three years, then I wouldn't count on it for the next."

"He's dead, isn't he?" Chrissa could not help herself. She stared straight at her grandmother, and in that split second, saw the old woman's eyes fill with tears. For a moment Gram's mouth seemed to be tugging down at the corners, but she quickly reached for her water glass.

"Of course not," she said.

Okay, he was dead. Gram might as well have come right out with it. Chrissa would ask no more questions, but she would search. Oh, how she would search! Dad's things were here somewhere; she could start with those. With all the bags and boxes in the spare bedroom.

She wrote out a grocery list for Gram the next morning.

"I've left my number by the phone," her grandmother

said, pulling up her support hose. "Mondays, Wednesdays, and Fridays I look in on Mrs. Hagerty mornings, Mr. Banks in the afternoons. Tuesdays and Thursdays I take care of this little baby down in Dansville. All the numbers are there, you need to reach me. I'll be home at five with the groceries, and you'll find enough for lunch, if you look."

"All right." Chrissa waited. Then, "Anything else you want me to do?"

"Tidy the kitchen—do what needs doing. We'll work out a schedule this week. And you can start on that reading list anytime. A whole lot of books on that list, Chrissie."

Gram stood up, made sure her house dress was zipped to the top, and—carrying a large canvas tote bag—headed for the car. She stopped halfway out the door. "If I hear of anyone wanting a sitter, I'll let you know."

It was a relief to have Gram out of the house. Chrissa ate quickly. Forget the kitchen. Except for a few old tea and coffee tins that held odds and ends on top of the refrigerator, there was nothing of interest there. A calendar beside the refrigerator had a few names and phone numbers on it, but no mention of a visit from Nick Jennings. Chrissa checked every month of the year. No Nick. No N.J.

The dining room. A high glass-front china cabinet with a collection of antique sugar bowls, and cups stacked in teetering rows with an unused look.

Living room. Tufted maroon-velvet furniture that looked like large fat men with shirts bulging at the buttons. A maroon-and-gray rug, worn through in places. A low bookcase with a collection of mystery novels, health manuals, and owl figurines, a desk . . .

34

Chrissa sat down in her rumpled T-shirt to check out the desk drawers. Bess and Shadow situated themselves in the doorway and watched with green eyes.

The first drawer on the left contained writing paper. She checked each drawer in turn. Receipts and bank statements in another. The third was full of pamphlets on health and religion. Fourth drawer: locked.

She tried again, giving it a tug in case it was only stuck. Locked. Definitely locked.

She stood up, pushing the chair back exactly as she'd found it, and went upstairs. Forget the spare bedroom for now. She went into Gram's instead.

A picture of Jesus and an old photo of President Kennedy hung on the wall above the bed, along with a two-year-old calendar that had a picture of three kittens in a basket. Gram's shoes—her ugly shoes—were lined up along one wall as though preparing to march in formation. And in the closet her drab dresses hung limply from the hangers, shoulders dropping off sharply at both ends.

Chrissa had to be careful not to rearrange a thing. The closet door was open an inch, and it would have to be in that same position when Gram came home. She turned on the light in the closet. There were shoeboxes and hatboxes that probably held neither shoes nor hats. A couple of old purses, an umbrella with missing handle, blankets . . .

She decided to start with the boxes and had just lifted one down when she thought she heard a noise. The thud of a door closing. She listened without breathing. Nothing.

Still holding the shoebox, she moved halfway across the floor, listening again. Still nothing. She opened the box and looked inside. Shoulder pads. An entire shoebox filled with mismatched shoulder pads.

35

The noise again. Footsteps. Chrissa set the shoebox on the bed and moved across the floor to the doorway.

There was Sister Harmony, coming rapidly up the stairs.

6

"Well!" Sister Harmony stopped, catching her breath, and then, uninvited, kept climbing.

Chrissa stepped backward as the large woman reached the top of the stairs. "I didn't hear you knock," she said.

"Didn't you, now? Don't have a radio on, do you?"

"No."

"Is your grandmother here?"

"She's working."

"That's her room, isn't it?"

Chrissa stared as Sister Harmony moved past her and took a few steps into Gram's bedroom. The woman wanted an answer: "What were you doing in her room?"

"I . . . I was . . ."

The preacher pursed her mouth. "Now, Chrissa, we both know why you were sent here to your grandmother's. She's only out of the house an hour, and already you—"

Chrissa could hardly get her voice. "Why did you come, then? I mean . . . if you knew she wasn't here?"

This time five seconds passed before Sister Harmony answered, and then her expression took on a softer look. "Why, I came to see you! Just wanted to get acquainted."

"I was looking for shoulder pads for one of my jackets," Chrissa lied, going back into Gram's room. She began sorting through them as though looking for two the same size, but her heart was still pounding.

"Then I'm sorry I misjudged you," Sister Harmony said amicably. "I do apologize, Chrissa. Do you think I might have a cup of tea while I'm here? I'm out making rounds."

"I could heat up the breakfast coffee."

"Would you?"

Sister Harmony followed her downstairs and settled herself on a kitchen chair, feet planted firmly on the floor, digging in. She rested her round arms on the table, waiting while Chrissa turned on the flame under the pot.

There was something about this woman. . . . Chrissa not only disliked but feared her. Minutes, it seemed, went by in silence, but as she poured the coffee, Chrissa got up her nerve and asked, "What else has Gram told you about me?"

Sister Harmony raised her cup to her mouth, blew on it, and set it down again without tasting. "Not a word escapes Elvina's lips that isn't meant to help someone." She smiled. "I want us to be friends, Chrissa, and I'm afraid we started out on the wrong foot."

It seemed impolite to be standing, so Chrissa poured a glass of orange juice and sat down across from the woman.

"Not much to do here for a girl your age, is there?" Sister Harmony asked. "I've been preaching around New York State for two years now, and I see the young people all heading for the cities. Round here they go to Rochester. Kodak, you know." She cradled her cup in her hands.

"Do you always hold your services in a tent?"

"Well, the Lord says that when two or three are gathered

38

together in His name, there He is also. I'm all over the county, you see. Six different towns."

"But what do you do in winter?"

"Rent out halls somewhere. Last year I was preaching in a room at the Elks Club, an Arthur Murray studio, two restaurants, and a warehouse. The Lord provides. I sure could use another pair of hands on Wednesdays and Sundays, though. Would you be willing to help out?"

"What would I do?"

"Set up the folding chairs, pass out the hymn sheets."

"Well . . . I'm not sure. Is it a . . . paying job?"

Sister Harmony was clearly shocked. "Why, my girl, you'd hardly expect me to *give* you something. . . ."

God loves a cheerful giver, Chrissa thought, and wished she had the courage to say it aloud. "I'll see," she said.

For a while after Sister Harmony left, Chrissa felt too cowed to go back upstairs. It was as though the woman in white could see her even when she wasn't there. She waited until her pulse felt normal, then locked both front and back doors before going to Gram's room again.

There was nothing of interest in Gram's dresser drawers—empty medicine bottles, eyeglass cases, discarded gloves with soiled fingertips: the dull accumulations of an old woman who had nothing more precious to fill the space.

The work was tedious, made worse by Chrissa's attention to putting everything back exactly as it had been. But when she heard Gram's car pulling up, she managed to be at the back door, holding it open, as Gram came in with groceries.

Later, sitting beside Gram on the swing by the pond, Chrissa said, "Sister Harmony was here today. Walked right in and up the stairs. I could have been stark naked."

Gram chuckled. "She'll do that way. You don't come to the door first time she knocks, she's liable to walk on in."

"How long have you been going to her tent meetings?"

"Most of two months now, ever since I heard the testimonials on how she heals. I've never been much good at churches, Chrissie. But I keep thinking Sister Harmony's doing these knees of mine some good. Oh, look!" Her thin hand clutched Chrissa's. "Up there. See?"

Chrissa looked up at a small dark object zigzagging this way and that, low over the pond, coming once or twice in their direction, then backtracking in no particular pattern that Chrissa could make out.

"What is it?"

"Bat."

Instantly Chrissa ducked, hands over her head, face in her lap, and this time Gram laughed aloud. Leaned forward, then reared back, lifting her slippered feet off the ground. "It's not going to get in your hair, Chrissie! I swear to God, I do nothing else, I'm going to take some of that city out of you and fill you with country before you go back."

Chrissa sat up warily, then gave another shriek and dived again as the bat returned, and this time Gram went into rolling laughter, until the swing jiggled and shook.

Chrissa laughed a little too. "Well, I always *heard* they got in your hair. . . ."

"I don't know when I've been so tickled!" gasped Gram.

Chrissa liked the feeling between them just then.

◆ ◆ ◆

Chrissa was sitting on the floor in the hallway, holding two pan lids. Rain pelted down on the roof of the apartment building, and

Chrissa watched the windows expectantly. Every time lightning flashed, she banged the pan lids—three, four, even five times—to drown out the thunder that followed. Gram taught her to do that.

She hardly knew her father was there, watching over the top of his magazine, until once, when a crack of thunder caught her unaware and she jumped, then banged the lids together as hard as she could, she saw him smile.

"You're a funny little kid," he said.

She was warmed by his smile. He liked her, then, and thought she was funny. She smiled back in spite of the thunder, and when she banged the lids once again, he laughed out loud. The smile and the laughter sustained her all week, long after he left again on Friday.

◆ ◆ ◆

When the bat had gone, Chrissa straightened up and said, somewhat chagrined, "I still don't much like it here."

"You don't *have* to like it, Chrissa. You only have to put up with it. When school starts, you'll make friends."

"You're an optimist, Gram."

"Life is full of surprises," Gram told her.

They sat and swung, Gram picking up the slack when Chrissa's feet slowed, Chrissa pushing when she sensed Gram tiring. Like a tandem bike, she thought.

"Now. Tell me what you did today. Want a full report. You started any of those books yet?" Gram asked.

"Not yet."

"Well, I got a whole line-up of things to keep you busy. Like to sew? We could pick up some cotton for skirts. And I bought one of those hair magazines—Fourteen Ways to Wear Your Hair This Summer—though I wouldn't want any of 'em tried on me. Got some beads that need stringing."

41

"Maybe," said Chrissa. The woman was trying.

Gram got up finally to walk around the pond, then went inside. A light came on in the house, making a square of yellow on the grass. Here and there a firefly flitted over the pond. For a moment, a fleeting moment, Chrissa felt as though she had been transported somewhere—transformed into something new, a chrysalis perhaps. Chrissa, the Chrysalis.

It was a feeling she had never quite experienced before, and she tried to cling to it, to conjure it up again, but it was too fleeting, and passed.

Next on the agenda: find out what was in the locked desk drawer. Find out where Gram kept the key.

7

Besides Sister Harmony, the other person Chrissa didn't care for was the piano player. Gram talked her into going to the Wednesday night prayer meeting. The crowd was small but earnest, and some of the requests were so personal that they were handed to Sister Harmony on little slips of paper. The large woman in the white dress held them in her cupped hands and did a generic prayer to cover them all.

While Sister Harmony was praying, the piano player—Sister Harmony's nephew, Gram had told her—unwrapped a stick of gum. Chrissa saw that he had a tattoo on the back of one hand, the outline of a bucking bronco. He wore a string tie, the kind cowboys wore. *Cowboys for Christ?* Chrissa wondered, and smiled at the thought.

She was always smiling at the wrong time. Again she noticed Sister Harmony watching, even as she led the small group in prayer. Chrissa immediately dropped her eyes to her lap, moving her wrist just enough to see her watch. Forty-five minutes to go.

"I don't think I want to come to these tent meetings any-more," she said on the way home.

"Why not?"

"Sister Harmony and her nephew give me the creeps."

Gram studied her a moment. "Suit yourself," she said.

On Saturday, Gram drove her to Ontario Beach, and they found an outdoor concert to attend that evening—bought sandwiches. Gram suggested other places they might go—a trip through the Kodak plant, museums, Niagara Falls even.

But this only made Chrissa more aware of the fact that she had no friends her own age up here. She watched other young people joking among themselves and having a good time. What if some of these kids turned up in her classes and remembered her going around Rochester with her grandmother?

She began tackling the spare bedroom while Gram was gone during the day. It would take weeks to go through every bag, every box, piled as they were on bed and chairs, leaving only a narrow path from door to closet. It was also the hottest room in the house, especially during the day, but how could she go the rest of her life not knowing?

All she had found in the rest of the house were small jars of assorted buttons, packages of pipe cleaners, a cigar box of wooden spools—the kinds of things she would save if she were still baby-sitting Bobby Westfall.

She began with the boxes of Dad's things that Mom had once sent. They were still taped shut, as though Gram couldn't bear to open them. Chrissa tried to slit the tape unobtrusively, and guiltily went through the pockets of her father's suits and jackets. Matches, a shirt button, receipts for lunch, loose change. Nothing remarkable.

Where was his wallet? What happened to his car? No answers here.

Still, while Chrissa had the clothes in her hands, she

44

brought a bundle to her face and drank in their scent. The after-shave still lingered. Even the musk smell of his deodorant clung to his shirts. She could not get enough of him, perhaps because she'd had so little.

◆ ◆ ◆

Chrissa knew the pattern now. Casually stretching by the open window, her father announced his departure. "Well, I'll be taking off tomorrow, I guess."

Her mother's hurt look. "You just got here, Nick!"

"I'm a working man." He lit a cigarette.

"But I thought . . . this weekend maybe . . ."

"You trying to call the shots, babe? You think I want to come back to this each time I go off?"

"No, but I miss you when you're gone so much."

"Miss you too, babe. Back before you can say Jack Robinson."

It didn't work. Chrissa sat on her bed saying "Jack Robinson" a dozen times and it never brought him back any sooner. He was always the fairy-tale father, promising more than he could deliver.

"Sure, we'll go to the beach some weekend." Or, "We'll get down to Florida one of these days. Go to Disney World—do it up big." Or, "Going to move out of this city—buy a house on the ocean. That's where you belong, Chrissa." For a long time she lived on promises, until she discovered how hungry she was and how little they sustained her.

After he left, Mom would retreat to her magazines and Chrissa retreated inside herself. They were both hurting, but the hurt never made it into words. Then the magical phone call a week, two weeks, even a month later, that Nick was coming home, and their spirits revived.

Lorraine sang and joked. She did something different with her hair, and together they danced to show tunes on the radio. Life on

Nineteenth Street revolved around Nick's comings and goings. He was their sun, and the apartment was warm or cold, depending on whether or not he was there. That was the scary part—their needing him.

◆ ◆ ◆

It was a relief to escape outside. Gram had been right—the pond never looked the same twice, but took its cue from the color of the sky, the strength of the breeze. Sometimes it was smooth as the blade of a knife; other times the surface had a ruffled, crepe-like appearance, like the skin around Gram's eyes. Or perhaps it was clear and dark, and Chrissa, bending over, could make out a goldfish lurking near the bottom. There were days it disguised itself by becoming a mirror for the sky, and Chrissa could watch the clouds by looking down.

Chrissa began taking Gram's field guide out to the swing to see how many birds she could identify. She had already seen a purple finch, starling, robin, two kinds of sparrows, chickadee, and grackle. On one particular day she had just added a blue jay to the list when she heard the sound of a car pulling in off the road. She stopped swinging to see who would emerge from behind a line of fir trees along the drive.

"Not *her* again!" she said aloud as a white Buick came into view. It moved slowly up to the end of the gravel and stopped. The piano player.

Chrissa sat still as a stone and watched as the man planted one pointy-toed shoe on the ground, then the other. Sister Harmony's nephew stood up slowly, a tall man in a dark suit, leaning against the open door of his car.

Despite the smile on his face, Chrissa did not think she had ever seen a man look more sinister. It was the way he

46

came uninvited, for one thing. He knew Gram wasn't here.

He thinks I'm going to invite him in, he figured wrong, Chrissa told herself.

"Afternoon." The man walked over and stood in front of her, feet apart, like a cowboy. Except that he was dressed more like an undertaker. Only the string tie and sideburns seemed out of place.

Chrissa slowly began swinging again. "Hi," she said, and looked past him towards the woods. She was thinking of what she might use as a weapon if necessary.

"Enjoying the breeze, I see," the man said, never taking his eyes off her.

She didn't answer.

"When's the last time you came to see your grandma?"

"I don't remember," Chrissa lied.

The piano player took a package of gum from his pocket and offered her a stick. Chrissa shook her head. "Well, it's a good thing you didn't see her a couple months ago. She's a whole lot better than she was."

Chrissa glanced up. His was a long stretched-out kind of face, with extra space between his nostrils and upper lip. Only the eyes were close together. "Why? What was the matter with her?" Chrissa asked.

"You tell me." He coolly unwrapped a stick for himself and put it in his mouth, eyes on her all the while. "But Sister Harmony improved her a hundred percent. Elvina's got that old spring back in her step."

"She never told me she was sick."

"She wouldn't. Take a hurricane to bring Ma Jennings down, but she was sinking, no doubt about it. Sister Harmony got her to talking, and you could almost see the color come back in Ma Jennings' face."

What does he expect me to do, applaud? Chrissa wondered. Why was he telling her this?

"So . . ." the piano player went on. "Thought you ought to know. She's doing well, and we want to keep her that way. Anytime you need us, just call, day or night."

Chrissa gave no answer.

Now he was studying her intently, and gave a little laugh. "You're the talkative one, aren't you!"

She shrugged. "I just can't think of anything to say." She hated the dry, wispy way her words came out.

"Oh, there's plenty, you feel like it," he said.

"Well, I've got things to do," Chrissa told him, picking up her field guide and notebook.

He was standing right in front of her, however, like a neighborhood bully, and at first Chrissa thought he wasn't going to move. Then he wadded up his gum wrapper, tamped the tinfoil into a tight little ball with his fingers, and tucked it back in his pocket.

"See you around," he said, and went back to his car.

Chrissa watched, her mouth feeling dry, as the Buick disappeared behind the line of fir trees.

"That piano player was here," she told Gram at dinner.

"Sister Harmony's nephew?" Gram scooped up a bite of peas. "What'd he want?"

"I'm not sure. Said you hadn't been doing so well before you met Sister Harmony."

"That's the Lord's truth," said Gram. "That woman gives me hope, Chrissie. Best medicine there is."

"I just wish they wouldn't come when you're not here."

"Well, I'll tell them if that's how you feel. They only want to look in on you, be helpful. Maybe they can

48

work the same magic on you they worked on me."

"I'd rather they didn't try," said Chrissa.

Two trunks arrived from home, with Chrissa's fall and winter clothes in them, boots, more underwear and more shoes . . . It was official then, Chrissa's exile. In all the spare spaces Mom had stuffed paperback novels, cosmetic samples, popcorn . . . There was also a letter:

Dear Chrissa,

I went through your room twice and can't see anything else you couldn't get by without. Tell me if you need something more and I'll send it.

I'm keeping busy. Things are pretty much the same at the office, but I've been getting out a little. Remember David, from the office? He has season tickets to the theater, and I've really been enjoying that. We may drive out to Long Island for the Fourth.

Hope things are going well at Gram's. If you feel like it, let me hear from you now and then.

Love,
Mom

July. Every few days Chrissa had been going deeper into Gram's woods. She was determined to walk all the way through to the other side, just to say she could.

There was no path: That was the unsettling part. Chrissa memorized the landmarks in the order she met them so she could find her way back home again: the fallen tree with mushrooms at the base, the peeling birch, the brook . . .the air was cooler with every step she took. Twenty or so feet into the trees, her skin even turned to gooseflesh.

She had discovered the bog that Gram talked about—a dark, dank place where ferns thrived—rich-smelling to her nostrils. She had to detour far around to keep from sinking down. Yet each time she went a little farther, and her eyes sought out things she had not noticed before.

Already she'd begun bringing home wildflowers from the woods as proof, if only to herself, that she had been there.

"Why, you've got some wild sarsaparilla there," Gram might say, or exclaim over cow wheat or yellow slipper.

On this afternoon Chrissa had dressed in cutoffs and a cotton shirt, knotted at the waist. She had been walking for some time—scrambling, actually—because each step was not so much a stride as a climb over dead branches and stumps. With each step she had to part the bushes on either side of her, looking out for thorns and spiny stems. Then she would put the next foot down.

She was farther than she had ever been before, way beyond the bog, and had just glimpsed open sky ahead when she heard a loud, piercing sound like a horn or a trumpet.

HONK! HONK, HONK, HONK, HONK HONK!

HONK! Honk, honk, honk, *honk, honk, honk* . . .

She stood motionless, pulse pounding, eyes huge. Animal or bird? The sound was repeated—a series of loud sharp blasts, all on the same note, followed by notes going halfway down the scale, over and over again.

Nothing moved. Chrissa could feel a trickle of sweat down her back. The strange noise went on and on.

And suddenly the honking took on a different sound. This time the notes went all the way down the scale and dissolved into grunting, gabbling, grumbling kinds of noises that rose and fell, rose and fell; went halfway back up the scale again as though they might be music after all, then fell into their quarrelsome complaints.

One animal or two? Chrissa looked all around her for clues. No tracks in the damp earth that she could detect. She heard no rustle of leaves, saw no moving branches.

Maybe there was something penned up on the property just ahead. *Show a little spunk.* She took a few steps forward, making her way over another tangle of vines and leaves.

The noise stopped suddenly, and Chrissa with it. Silence. Dead calm.

Now what? She took a step forward again.

HONK! HONK, HONK, HONK . . .

She stepped out onto the edge of a field and stared. A boy, probably fifteen, stood leaning against a shed no more than ten yards away. He was holding something to his lips—an instrument, it seemed, about the size of a tonette. Cupping his hands over the end of it, he alternately pressed and raised his fingers as he blew, sometimes barely uncovering the end, sometimes exposing the whole thing.

The noise stopped a second time and the boy stared back.

"Well!" he said. "Look what I caught!"

8

Chrissa tried to step backward, but her foot was trailing a vine. The blood rose to her face.

He grinned at her. "Taking a shortcut or something?"

"No, not really." She bent down to untangle her foot.

"Am I supposed to guess, then?" the boy asked. "Twenty questions?"

Her face burned brighter still. *This stupid vine!* "Just out walking," she said.

"I'm Thad Hewlitt. Live in the house up there." He gave a nod toward a farmhouse farther on. "You staying at Ma Jennings' place?"

"Yes." She actually had to slip her sneaker off to get herself loose, then worked at trying to put it on again standing up.

Now the boy was laughing. "Could I help? Or would you like to sit down?"

Chrissa gave up finally and limped over to a log. She laughed too. "I'm Chrissa Jennings."

"Ma Jennings' granddaughter, I'll bet. Hi, Chrissa."

"What *is* that thing?" she asked.

He held up the instrument. "Duck call. Just practicing."

She didn't have any idea what he was talking about.

"You staying for the concert or just passing through?" he asked, smiling. He was about six feet tall, wide shouldered yet lanky, with a bank of fine eyebrows that came together over the bridge of his nose.

"I just wanted to see what was on the other side of the woods," she told him.

"Go take a look if you want, but I'll guarantee it's nothing interesting."

"Well, I'll go back, then." Chrissa started to get up.

"She's *not* staying for the concert!"

Chrissa smiled. "Okay, I'll listen."

"That's more like it. How long you going to be here?"

"A year, I guess."

"No kidding? You'll go to school, then. All the buses stop out on the road between your place and mine."

Chrissa could tell that this little spot between the trees and shed was a place that Thad came to often. It had the trampled-down look that made it seem friendly, cast completely in shade. The log she was sitting on, in fact, had names and initials carved on top.

"This is your favorite place?" she asked.

"One of them," Thad told her. "Anytime Dad doesn't need me, I come out here and practice my calls."

Chrissa stretched out her legs and rested the palms of her hands on the log on either side of her. A red-winged blackbird, the first she had seen, flew in over the field and perched on a wheat shaft that slowly bent double beneath its weight. "So where are the ducks?" she asked. "I mean, are you like a shepherd or something? A duck keeper?"

Thad laughed and looked astonished. "Where you from?"

53

"New York City."

"Figures." He chuckled some more. "Dad and I go duck hunting every fall. If I'm lucky, I can lure in a few. Geese, too, but I need more practice with that. Want to hear some calls?"

"Sure."

Thad raised the duck call to his lips, his fingers closing over the end, and tipped his head back.

HONK! HONK, HONK, HONK, HONK, HONK . . .

The sound this close was horrendous. Chrissa couldn't remember ducks making any noise other than an occasional quack—the ducks she'd seen in Central Park, anyway. But when Thad moved down the scale and the notes got softer, more conversational than quacking, she could well imagine a flock of gabbling, quarrelsome ducks mistaking the sounds for a flock enjoying themselves on a lake below.

Eyes intent, Thad focused on a spot just beyond Chrissa and went through the repetitions again, fingers moving over the end of the call, head and body tipping and swaying, turning first one way, then another, which made the sound itself rise and fall, rise and fall. It came from one direction, then another.

He stopped mid-scale.

"That's all?" Chrissa asked.

Thad grinned. "Red light."

"What?"

He laughed. "That means 'stop,' when you're competing. You only have a minute and a half after the warm-up to do your routine."

She looked at him blankly. "Where do you compete?"

"Waterfowl festivals. Ever hear of them?"

Chrissa shook her head.

"I enter the regionals each year. Usually come home with at least some twelve-gauge shells or something as a prize." He let his knees bend, back sliding down the side of the shed until he was sitting on the ground across from her. "So how come you're here at your grandmother's?"

Chrissa shrugged. "Mom and I weren't getting along so well." She trapped a weed between her sneakers and worked at trying to pull it up. "She thinks a year away from each other might clear the air."

"Oh."

The weed came up and Chrissa ground it back into the earth with her shoe. "What are the schools like?"

"Some of the teachers are good, some are a little nuts. The high school's got a good band—good newspaper. Lousy football team, though."

"You the only one in your family?"

"I've got a married brother, but he lives nearby. Dad would like me to stay here on the farm, of course, but I want to go to college. Think it over. I like the out-of-doors, but I like music, too. Computers. Too many things I like. What do you like?"

Chrissa tried to think. TV? Shopping? Baby-sitting? Talking to Gram?

"Trees," she said at last, surprising even herself.

"Trees?" Was he laughing at her?

"I like Gram's yard. The pond, the trees . . . I like walking out here in the woods when it's hot."

"I know. That's why I do my calls here. Mom says the farther away from the house, the better." He was looking right at her again. "So how old are you?"

She blushed again. "Thirteen."

55

"Only thirteen?" His eyes were laughing. "A kid, huh?"

"I won't call you 'farm-boy' if you don't call me 'kid,'" she told him.

"Deal."

There was a far-off whistle. Thad got up. "Dad needs me. See you around?"

"See you," Chrissa replied, and headed back through the woods. But she went only a few yards before she turned and watched him go. Watched his lanky frame loping across the field toward the house. She was embarrassed when he turned suddenly and looked at her, and she wheeled around again and quickly headed for Gram's.

◆ ◆ ◆

From the fifth-floor apartment on Nineteenth Street, she watched him throw his bag on the seat and drive off. He didn't look up and he didn't wave. Her father often omitted the wave when he'd be gone only a short while. This time would be different, but Chrissa didn't know it then.

◆ ◆ ◆

When she reached Gram's place fifteen minutes later, she went down to the mailbox. Every day she intercepted the mail before Gram got to it, in case Dad had written. Once again there was no letter from him, either for her or Gram. Only the electric bill, Gramp's pension check, and a newsletter from Sister Harmony called *"Harmonious Living"*: *"Give to God more than you believe you possibly can, and He will reward you with more than you ever deserved."*

There were almost no visitors, other than Sister Harmony on occasion, and a yard man who came by every other week with a tractor mower. Elvina Jennings lived so

56

far out in the country that her friends consisted of the ladies of the Bingo Club at the firehouse, and two old friends from Rochester whom she visited now and then.

Gram opened *"Harmonious Living"* when she got home and found a little envelope and card stapled between the pages. Sister Harmony's name was stamped on the envelope, with an Albany post-office box. Chrissa could read the card from where she sat. There was a picture of a nail file with the words JESUS SAVES printed on it, and a short message:

Many of you have contributed to the Whole Body Church of the Lord for several years. What a wonderful reward you have waiting for you in heaven! I feel a holy power for healing for each and every member of our congregation. But prices have gone up, and the Lord needs your contributions. Send today for the lovely nail file, free with each offering. Check the amount of your gift below:

$5_____ $10_____ $20_____   More_____

"Twenty dollars for a nail file?" Chrissa choked.

Gram sat fingering the card. "Thought I sent her some money not long ago; maybe it was longer than I thought."

"How much did you give last time she sent an envelope?"

"Well, now, that's my business, isn't it?"

"Sorry," Chrissa said quickly. And then, "How do you know she helps you?"

"My knees tell me. Last April that left knee of mine hurt so bad it was like someone hitting at it with a hammer. But

I walked down to the mailbox and back last week, and all I felt was a twinge. Now that's healing!"

"Might have been the weather," Chrissa offered. And when Gram frowned, she said, "I met the boy who lives on the other side of the woods. Thad Hewlitt. Do you know him?"

"Sure I know the Hewlitts. Mr. Hewlitt's the one who put in the pond for me." Gram studied her. "How did you come to see him?"

Chrissa explained about walking through the woods.

Gram listened, lips pursed. "If he ever comes over to see you, you'll entertain him in the yard, of course," she said finally. "Unless I'm home."

"*Entertain* him? what do you want me to do? Sing and dance?" Chrissa said.

Gram held back a smile. "If he comes courting, young lady."

"Courting?" Chrissa stared. "Gram, I met this boy this one time for maybe ten minutes, and we're *courting*?"

"Well, what*ever* you call it, if he *does* come over, he's not to come in unless I'm here."

"It wouldn't even occur to me to invite him in."

Gram leaned back in her chair, hands in her lap. "What *do* you do all day, Chrissie?"

"Read, walk in the woods, sit out on the swing and watch the birds, cook, dust, bake cookies, wash my stuff, listen to tapes, watch TV . . ." Chrissa added every possible activity to the list to cover up for the time she spent searching for her father's address.

"Doesn't seem enough, somehow, you figure I'm gone sometimes eight, nine hours at a stretch." Gram lowered her head and looked at Chrissa over the rim of her glasses.

"I left you that list of what I expect from you while you're here, but I didn't say a word about . . . well, drink and drugs and . . ." She paused, and Chrissa couldn't help but grin.

"Sex," she said. Did she only imagine it, or was there pink in Gram's cheeks all of a sudden?

"That, too," Gram said hurriedly. "I don't allow any of that in this house. Not that I don't trust you, Chrissie, but I don't want *any*one coming in here while I'm away."

"I hope you'll tell that to Sister Harmony," said Chrissa.

She was thinking of Thad again as she and Gram sat before the TV that evening, watching the news. She'd made only one friend so far, but it *was* nice to know the name of at least one person around her age.

During a commercial, when Gram reached down to pull off her shoes, Chrissa noticed something slip out of the neck of her cotton dress and dangle a moment before Gram's finger reached up and deftly tucked it back in place.

A key. In that second Chrissa had seen it shining. And in that same second she knew that this was the key to the drawer that might tell her what all the other drawers in the house could not.

She waited until Gram was in the bathtub later, then stole quickly into her grandmother's room, looking for the key on her dresser. It wasn't there. Gram seemed to have taken off her clothes in the bathroom. And when she came down to the living room later, her gray hair wet around the edges, the liver spots standing out on the dry white skin of her face, Chrissa could see the key gleaming on its chain just inside the collar of her robe.

9

The first real quarrel between Chrissa and Gram happened the following Saturday. Realizing she'd forgotten to add some items to the previous Monday's grocery list, Chrissa decided to walk to the Seven Eleven. It couldn't be more than a mile to the highway, and would save her the lecture on planning ahead.

Gram kept their grocery money in an envelope on the counter, so Chrissa slipped it into the pocket of her shorts. Then, while Gram was napping about two, Chrissa set off down the sloping drive to the highway.

It was more like a two-mile walk, she discovered, and would have been unbearable if the weather were hot. The sky was overcast, however, and Chrissa liked being away from the house, out in the world of truck drivers and deliverymen speeding by her on the road. She was too closed-in at Gram's, and found herself longing for school.

At the store she kept her purchases to a minimum, but still, when she remembered the cereal she wanted and the napkins that were needed, the groceries filled up two sacks. She chose paper because Gram insisted on it, but had not gotten a hundred yards away when she wished she'd chosen plastic. The sacks weren't as heavy as they were cumbersome.

She would walk quicker, she decided, taking longer strides—get home before her arms gave out. She practiced letting the bags rest on her hip bones, an arm encircling each bag halfway round. But still, after only a few minutes, her arms and shoulders ached. She put the sacks on the ground for a moment to rest, then started off again.

The road stretched endlessly before her, and she was dismayed to see the yellow barn, which she had decided was the halfway point, was still far off in the distance.

This was one of the stupidest things she had ever done. She stopped and held up a knee, resting one of the sacks on it, and, as she did so, heard the sound of a vehicle pulling onto the shoulder behind her. She turned.

A man leaned out the window of a van. He appeared to be in his late thirties—deep-set eyes, wrinkled shirt. "Look like you could use a ride," he called.

Chrissa studied him, sweat running down her face. She didn't dare. "Oh, I'm okay, I think."

"Doesn't look like it. One of those bags is starting to give. I'm on my way to the gas station. Hop in."

Chrissa looked down. The left bag was beginning to split where a can of frozen orange juice soaked through.

Darn!

"How far you going?" the man asked.

"Elvina Jennings' place. It's another mile, I guess."

"Come on. I'll drive you to the door."

Did she dare? All her mother's warnings came back to her, but her arms said yes, and she saw there was no other way to get the groceries home. She remembered a stop sign a half mile beyond Gram's. If the man didn't turn in at the driveway, she'd jump out when they reached the intersection.

She walked back to the van, hunched protectively over the ripping bag, and pushed the sack onto the seat ahead of her, between herself and the driver. Then, holding the other bag, she climbed in.

"Thanks," she said.

He inched the car forward, waiting for a break in traffic, then moved out onto the road.

Chrissa glanced over at his gas gauge. Two-thirds full. Her heart beat faster. She gave him a quick look.

"You don't want to try this very often," he said. "No telling who might pick you up. If I hadn't offered you a ride, you might not have been so lucky with the next guy."

It was not reassuring somehow.

The man reached forward and turned the radio on. "I could be just about anyone at all," he continued, over the country music that came through the speaker. "Rapist. Murderer. No telling what I might do." His voice sounded strange, sermonizing. On and on he went. Why pick her up and then scold her for getting in?

Chrissa felt more uneasy still. But when she pointed out Gram's drive, the car slowed and turned up the lane. Her shoulders sagged with relief.

"I got a delivery to make to a Mrs. Clyde Early. You happen to know where she lives?" the man asked.

"No," Chrissa said hurriedly, glad to be back.

The stranger pulled up to the house and slid her groceries across the seat toward her as Chrissa got out.

"You get someone to drive you next time, hear?"

"I will," Chrissa told him. "Thanks." She let out her breath.

He turned around, one arm on the back of the seat, and backed down the drive.

Gram was waiting at the door. "Who was *that*?" She stared at the car, then at the sacks in Chrissa's arms. "Who do you know with an Ohio license plate?"

"Just a man who gave me a ride home from the Seven Eleven. I guess I bought more things than I expected. I forgot to put these on the list."

"You don't even know who he was?" Gram's voice was high, tight.

"No, Gram. I thought I could make it home with the sacks, but I couldn't. One of them was ripping, and he stopped and offered, so I went."

Chrissa was stunned at the response. She had barely set the groceries down before Gram had her by one arm, a yardstick in her other hand, and was whacking at her legs.

"Don't you ever, never, let me catch you riding with a man you don't know!" Gram's face was pink.

"Gram!" Chrissa twisted away, but Gram came after her and whacked some more until Chrissa wrestled the yardstick away from her. There were red marks all up and down one calf. She stared in astonishment at her grandmother.

Gram leaned against the table breathing heavily. "Any girl raised in New York City ought to know better!"

Chrissa angrily threw the yardstick on the floor. "I don't like to be hit."

"Well, I don't like a girl under my roof who doesn't have the sense she was born with!" Gram declared. "You'll do any fool thing with a stranger, but let Sister Harmony and her nephew show a little kindness and you back off."

"What do *they* have to do with it?"

"You are under *my* care, Chrissa!" Gram continued, her

63

voice shrill. "All I want is what's best for you, and then you go off and try something like that."

"It's not as if I'd planned it."

Gram gave a snort. "Half the trouble in this world wasn't planned, girl! It just came upon folks who didn't have the sense to say no."

Chrissa turned on her heels and went upstairs, leaving the groceries untended. She had never seen her grandmother so upset. She in turn had never been so angry at Gram.

At six she went back down to prepare dinner. She expected some remorse on Gram's part, but the old woman gave her nothing of the kind—sat frowning over each bite she took, and it wasn't until almost nine o'clock, when she'd come in from the pond, that Gram seemed more herself again.

"*Chilly* out there," she said. "Sure doesn't feel like July."

This time it was Chrissa who gave no response.

◆ ◆ ◆

"Will Daddy be back in time for Christmas, because I know what I want to get him."

Mother was pouring bleach in the washing machine. "Don't get your hopes up," is what she said.

"But he's always been back by Christmas before."

"Like I said . . ."

"Why is he taking so long this time?"

"You're asking the wrong person."

"Well, I'm going to get him a present anyway."

"Suit yourself."

◆ ◆ ◆

It was on a Tuesday that she found the photo album. It was

in the third drawer of a short painted dresser blocked by a trundle bed piled high with old coats and boxes. It wasn't until Chrissa had sorted through all the boxes and moved the bed that she could get to the drawers of the dresser.

She should have known from the faded blue paint that this drawer was special. Should have known by the contents of the top drawer that it had once been in the bedroom of a little boy. There was an old yellow knit cap and booties, a cup with rabbits on it, a tattered stuffed dog with only one ear . . .

In the second drawer, by contrast, were old curtains, drapery hooks and rings. But in the third drawer, along with ancient songbooks and sheet music, was a photo album. When Chrissa opened the cover, which flaked off in her hand at the corners, she saw the name that someone had carefully inked in on the first page: *Nicholas Paul Jennings.*

It was too hot to look through it up in the bedroom, and she decided to take it downstairs and return it before Gram got home. There was a baby photo, undoubtedly her father, on the first page. It was hard to imagine Nick as a boy, much less a baby. To Chrissa it seemed he had always been the tall man with the sharply creased pants who arrived home with presents. Presents and a certain tension that made his going away again both a regret and a relief.

She bent down to check the last drawer of the dresser before she left the room, and saw only crumpled tissue paper—wads of paper stuffed into the drawer. Curious, she picked up a handful, and then her breath stopped. A gun.

For half a minute Chrissa stood like a statue, staring down at the gun—a silver handgun with black handle. She had never held a gun in her life, and had the crazy feeling that even standing so close to it might set it off. Gingerly, when her breath returned, she pulled out the rest of the tissue paper. No bullets. Nothing.

What could it mean? Was Gram uneasy about living out here and felt it necessary to have a gun? If so, she certainly would not keep it hidden away like this.

Gramps? Had it been his? Chrissa put the tissue paper back, closed the drawer, and went downstairs.

She put the scrapbook on the table to study while she drank a Coke, and was so absorbed in the photos that she didn't know Gram was home until she heard the car door slam.

As Chrissa leaped up, the scrapbook hit her cola bottle, knocking it from the table. She was wiping up the floor when Gram entered the kitchen.

The small slight woman stood in the doorway, her left foot resting outward on the side of her shoe taking in the cola on the floor and the scrapbook open on the table.

"I've made a mess," Chrissa said, wringing the dishcloth out in the sink and tackling the puddle again. And then, "I got so interested in these pictures, I forgot I had a Coke on the table."

Gram came on in and laid her keys on the counter. "Where did you find the album?"

"That little blue dresser in the spare bedroom. I thought maybe I could move it into my room to store some of my stuff." Well, she *might* need it, might she not?

"I suppose you could," said Gram. "Go down to the basement, Chrissa, and get the mop. The floor's still sticky over here."

As they shared some soup at the table later, Chrissa asked, "How come you're home for lunch?"

66

"Mrs. Sadoris quit her job to stay home with her baby, so now I've got Tuesdays and Thursdays to fill up again." Gram put her spoon down, then leafed through the mail she'd collected from the box. This time there was an envelope addressed to Chrissa with Sister Harmony's post office box in the upper left corner.

"Sister Harmony's been asking about you; sure would like to see your face sometime at service," Gram said, pushing the envelope toward Chrissa.

"Well, I sure wouldn't like to see hers," Chrissa retorted truthfully.

"Don't know why you take such a dislike to her."

"She's trying to sell *me* a nail file for twenty dollars, that's reason enough," Chrissa said. She opened the envelope.

There was no mention of a nail file, only a note:

Dear Chrissa:

Just want you to know I am praying for you daily. What's past is past, but think upon Jesus' own words: ". . . sin no more, lest a worse thing come unto thee." John 5:14.

Would love to see you at service on Wednesday. It would mean a great deal to your grandmother.

Sister Harmony

"How much does Sister Harmony know about me?" Chrissa asked. "Just what sin is she talking about?"

"I told her you and Lorraine weren't getting along."

"I wish you wouldn't talk to her about me."

"If that's what you want."

"It's what I want," Chrissa said.

Gram set about rinsing the dishes after lunch, but

Chrissa stayed at the table, looking through the scrapbook. There were baby photos of her father—on his back, on his stomach, sitting up, crawling—whatever a baby could be doing, there was a visual memory preserved in the book.

"Dad was a cute baby," she said at last.

"Yes, he was."

"You know what, Gram? I don't think I even remember what he looks like anymore. His face, I mean. If I was to meet him on the street, I'd probably pass right by."

Gram silently dried the spoons. "Would you, now?" she said, and put them in the drawer.

There was a thunderstorm that afternoon, and Chrissa, on the swing, watched it come. Far off, she heard a roll of thunder, like the growl of a sleeping dog who's been disturbed.

The breeze picked up, comforting and teasing at first, then more persistent, plucking at the sleeves of her shirt, whipping up her hair in back, tossing the tree branches down and around like the head of a balky horse.

The sun disappeared. Ten minutes before, there had been no clouds in the sky, and suddenly grayness swirled overhead—soup froth in a kettle.

A large drop of rain hit her hand. Another grazed her arm. The thunder had become a rumble now, like a truck out on the highway. Raindrops fell slowly, haphazardly, as the sky darkened even more. They struck the water of the pond randomly, each drop having its moment of glory as it created the perfect splash, eddies rippling out in concentric circles, one moving into the path of another and another.

Lightning. A large streak zigzagged across the sky in front of her. Chrissa blinked. She had never seen lightning so complete—the whole bolt, end to end.

Baaa-*room!* The thunder crashed and rolled, bouncing along, and kept rolling until it ended in its own echo.

The drops came faster now, splashing, pinging, thwacking as they struck water, metal or wood. Making its own music. A fresh damp smell rode in on the breeze.

Chrissa made a run for the house and watched from the porch as the sky grew black. Thunder crashed with deafening cracks and claps, and then rain came gushing down—sheets of rain, slantwise—giving the surface of the pond a thousand pockmarks, jiggling the leaves of the sycamore. The thing about rain, you had to accept it as it was. She wished she could feel the same about herself.

When it tapered off at last and the sun peeped through, everything glistened with water. The music of rain ended in a chorus of drops tapping lightly on the ground. Everything had been baptized with this rain of July, which had brought a healing to the hot dry brown of the countryside.

"I want to be like rain," Chrissa said as she pressed her nose against the screen and watched the storm move on.

She and Gram both walked to the woods that evening to look at the mushrooms growing near the bog. Gram picked the ones she was sure of and let the others be.

"If this was my woods, I'd build my house right in it," Chrissa said, relishing the damp.

Her remark seemed to make Gram wince.

"It's too big a woods for one person, Chrissie. I've no right keeping it all to myself."

"You're not! You're sharing it with me!" Chrissa laughed. "It's absolutely my favorite place!"

"Just seems a waste, somehow."

"Not to me."

When she went to bed that evening, Chrissa felt obliged to move the little blue dresser into her room as she'd told Gram she was going to do. She climbed over boxes again to get to the other side of the trundle bed, and pulled open the first drawer to empty its contents.

The drawer was empty. So was the second and third. When she opened the last drawer, it, too, stood empty. There was no telltale tissue paper strewn about the room either. The gun was gone.

10

When they went to the library on Thursday to get more books from her reading list, Chrissa waited till Gram was checking out new mysteries, then went to the reference desk.

"How can I find out if a person is living?" she asked.

"A famous person?"

"No."

"Here in New York State?"

"I . . . I guess so."

The librarian reached for a book from her shelf and looked up something in the index, then flipped the pages.

"Write to this address," she said, copying something down on her notepad and handing the sheet to Chrissa. "Give them all the information you have, and they'll tell you how to go about getting the death certificate, if there is one."

"Thank you." Chrissa tucked it in the pocket of her shorts. All she wanted was to know.

She returned the books she'd read so far at Gram's, and checked out *The Once and Future King, A Night to Remember,* and *The Scarlet Pimpernel*. That evening she wrote a letter to the Vital Records section at the state capital, and mailed it the following day after Gram left for work.

She wanted to see Thad again, and wished he'd call or come over. He probably thought she was too young, but twice she had gone through the woods again to his favorite place and found it empty.

Chrissa was tired of waiting, however. Waiting for Thad. Waiting to find out where her father was. Waiting for school. Her life was on hold. So with new resolve she set out a third time. If she even saw Thad off in the distance, she'd go talk to him. She followed the route she had begun for herself in the dense undergrowth, pleased to be the pioneer, her own feet making the winding path.

The day was overcast, and in the woods the shadows were black. It seemed as though bushes had turned into caves. Chrissa had gone perhaps a third of the way to the Hewlitts' when she thought she saw something move up ahead. She stopped and listened.

Twigs snapped. And then she heard voices. More than one person. Two, perhaps. Chrissa took a few steps more, then stopped and listened again.

". . . no, that's too high." Sister Harmony's voice! They were coming toward her.

The piano player: "A thousand? Wouldn't sell for less than a thousand. Sure of that."

What were they doing here in Gram's woods?

"Twelve hundred, maybe."

"Are you sure she said a hundred sixty acres? Woods seems bigger to me than that."

"That's what she told me. Unless she's holding back."

No! Chrissa stood with her hands over her mouth.

"Even at a thousand, we're talking a hundred sixty thousand bucks, Ruby."

Ruby? Sister Harmony was a ruby?

The piano player saw her about the same time Chrissa saw him. He stopped, and Sister Harmony, walking behind, bumped against him. He was clearly annoyed to see Chrissa.

"What'd you do, follow us in?" he asked.

Sister Harmony made her way around him, holding the bushes out away from her. There were burrs stuck to the laces of her crepe-soled shoes.

Chrissa's heart pounded fiercely. She wished her voice matched her anger: "It's Gram's woods," she said huskily. "She wouldn't sell it."

Sister Harmony, in her white uniform, smiled benevolently. "Why, Chrissa, we never said a word about your grandmother selling her woods. What she's doing is giving them to us after she leaves this earth."

"*Giving* them to you?" Chrissa gasped. "If they go to anyone, they should go to my dad. She's *his* mother!"

"If anything should happen to Elvina, Chrissa, her house would go to your father, of course. But your grandmother is a generous woman, and she's going to leave the woods to the Whole Body Church so we can have our own building. I knew it was an answer to prayer."

Tears welled up in Chrissa's eyes. "She wouldn't cut these trees down!"

"Neither would we! Only enough for a small church and parking lot. A retreat for body and soul."

"Gram could live a long time yet!" Chrissa declared. "It could be fifteen years before you could build anything."

"Indeed she could live a long time, and with God's help

73

she will," said Sister Harmony. "All we're doing is taking a walk, knowing that someday, here on this land, your grandmother's wish will come true." She looked about her and took a deep breath. "It's beautiful, isn't it? I can certainly see why you love it, and so will we."

Chrissa leaned against a tree, her breathing fast and shaky. Suddenly she rushed on toward the Hewlitts'. She couldn't let this happen! Gram must be out of her mind!

But once again, when she reached the place where Thad came to practice his duck calls, it was vacant. Far, far off in the distance, she could hear the sound of the tractor, but there was no one in sight.

She sat down on the log and bawled. If Thad heard her, she imagined, he'd say she sounded like a baby calf. But he didn't hear, and he didn't come. As sure as day, Sister Harmony wouldn't sit around for fifteen years waiting for Gram to die. She wanted that property now. And she and her nephew would sell it the minute their name was on the deed.

When Chrissa got up at last to go home, she knew that it wasn't enough just to find out what had happened to her father. If he was alive, she had to find him, let him know what was going on. He was the only one who could stop it.

The day before, Mom had called and talked with Gram. From what Chrissa could tell, it was the usual chatty conversation, but just before she hung up, Gram wrote down a phone number on the calendar. Chrissa didn't know whose number it was, but now, as she made her way home, she began to wonder if it could be her father's.

As soon as she got in the house, she went to the phone and dialed the operator.

"I want to make a collect call," she said. She didn't dare charge it to Gram's account. Her palms felt sweaty.

The phone rang and rang, but no one answered.

That night, after Gram had gone to bed, Chrissa crept downstairs. For several minutes she sat staring at the phone, one hand on the receiver, then drew a deep breath and tried again.

"A collect call," she told the operator.

The phone rang three and a half times, and then a man answered. Chrissa's heart leaped. It was a familiar voice.

"I have a collect call from Chrissa Jennings," the operator said. "Will you accept the charges?"

There was an awkward pause. The phone felt wet in Chrissa's hand.

"Chrissa? Well . . . certainly," the man said.

"Hi," Chrissa said softly. "It's me."

"Hello?" the man said again.

"It's Chrissa," she said again.

"I can hardly hear you."

Chrissa moved on around the corner, as far away from the stairs as she could get.

"It's Chrissa," she said again, a little louder.

"Chrissa! What's up? Anything wrong?"

Anything wrong? Is that all he had to say after three years?

"I can't talk too loud," she said. "Gram doesn't know I'm calling you."

"What's the matter?"

"I . . . I miss you," she said, hoping she wouldn't cry.

The pause. "Well . . . this is a surprise!"

"I wondered why you never came to see us. I mean, it's really been a long time."

"Well . . . not that long."

"Listen, do you think you could drive out here to Gram's? I've got to talk to you."

"Does your mother know you're calling me?"

"N-no."

"Isn't this something she should be able to handle?"

"No! It's about *you*! About Gram's woods. She's going to leave it to Sister Harmony in her will and—"

"Look. I'm seeing Lorraine tomorrow. Why don't I have her call you?"

"You're seeing Mom?"

"Of course. I mean, didn't you know?"

And suddenly Chrissa recognized the voice. It was not her father at all. It was David, from the office. Mom probably gave Gram the number in case there was an emergency and Gram couldn't reach her at home.

Her hand jerked forward and she dropped the phone. Oh, criminy!

Mother called the following evening.

"Chrissa, what in the *world*!"

Chrissa swallowed.

"Can you tell me what in heaven's name that was all about? Calling David at eleven at night?"

"It was a mistake, Mom."

"But why *David*?"

"I don't know. I was upset. Forget it, okay?"

There was a long silence. Finally Mother asked, "What's this about Gram selling her property?"

"She's not selling it; she wants to give her woods to this preacher she's met. She's putting it in her will."

"Chrissa, when Gram makes up her mind to do something, she does it."

"But I love these woods, Mom, and they should . . . should really go to Dad, shouldn't they?"

A pause. Lord, how Chrissa hated pauses.

"Like I said, Chrissa," Mother repeated, "Gram will do whatever she wants, and you and I don't have a thing to say about it."

11

First week of August.

"I saw Mrs. Hewlitt at her mailbox this afternoon," Gram told Chrissa on Friday, "and offered you to help out in her kitchen. Everything's coming ripe at the same time in her garden, and I told her you could go over tomorrow morning."

Chrissa gave her an indignant look, but inwardly she was pleased. "What if I have other plans?"

"Do you?"

"No, but—"

"Well, then! And Chrissa . . ." Gram stopped, choosing her words carefully, it seemed. "I wouldn't mention your father if I were you. Nick was a sore spot with them."

"Why? What happened?"

"Nothing happened. They just never got along. Thad will . . will *like* you better . . ." Even Gram seemed uncomfortable saying it . . . "if you don't talk about Nick."

Chrissa merely shrugged, but Gram needn't have worried. Why would Chrissa want Thad to know she had a father who hadn't come to see her for the past three years?

After breakfast the next day she put on a fresh T-shirt,

some lip gloss, and her father's Greek fisherman's cap, down low over her eyes.

"Chrissa," said Gram, when she came downstairs. "That's Nick's cap, isn't it?"

"Yes." Chrissa grinned. "What will the Hewlitts do? Ban me because of a cap? I happen to like it." She went out the door and headed for the woods.

Mrs. Hewlitt was a large woman with a wide face and a full smile, who met her at the door in a sleeveless dress that displayed the freckles on her arms. The house itself was surrounded by sunflowers.

"It's nice to watch something grow that I don't have to pickle, can, or freeze," was the way Thad's mother explained them. "Come on in, Chrissa. The men are picking peaches. Thad and his father have been up every day at five. Our busy season, you know."

In minutes, it seemed, Chrissa was sitting at the table snapping the ends off a half bushel of green beans at her feet, and listening to Mrs. Hewlitt's chatter. The beans were replaced by cucumbers that had to be sliced paper thin, covered with salt and ice cubes, and chilled in the refrigerator for pickle making.

"How long does this go on? All this canning?"

"Oh, we don't stop till Thanksgiving. I always fill my freezer first, but I do love a full pantry. Come see."

Carrying a box of her treasured jars, she led Chrissa down to the cellar where a coal bin had been converted to a pantry. Its shelves were half filled with tall jars of green beans, shiny jars of red tomatoes and yellow corn . . .

Chrissa liked the cellar—liked Mrs. Hewlitt, too, and couldn't imagine her not getting along with anyone, even Chrissa's father.

Upstairs again, Thad's mother asked polite questions about New York City as they sliced the cucumbers. How much did they pay for pork sausage back in the city? Was the fruit ripe when they bought it, or still green by the stem?

There were sounds from outside as the men returned for lunch, and Chrissa listened eagerly for Thad's voice. She had just stood up to carry another pan of cucumber slices to the refrigerator when the back door opened. Thad was preceded into the kitchen by a large black dog that headed straight for Chrissa, breaking into a trot.

Instantly, she sucked in her breath and backed up against the sink. "Th-thad!"

"Chrissa! Hey, easy! Midnight! Here, boy!" The dog came within an inch of Chrissa's thigh, then trotted back to Thad, tail wagging.

Chrissa let out her breath, face red.

"Okay, Midnight, give her back her leg," joked Thad's brother, and the laughter helped ease the awkwardness.

"Here this girl has been working her fingers to the bone, and you go and sic the dog on her!" Mrs. Hewlitt admonished good-naturedly.

"He's a Labrador, Chris," Thad explained, holding the dog's collar with one hand, patting its head with the other. "You can pet him if you like. Gentle as a kitten."

Chrissa shook her head and put her pan in the refrigerator.

"And the best hunting dog I ever had," Mr. Hewlitt put in. "You must be Ma Jennings' granddaughter."

She nodded, still embarrassed, but by the time the meal was on the table, she found that she was enjoying the banter, liked the feel of elbows crowding in on her as they sat down to fresh corn and beans and ham.

"Thad, you wash those hands?" his mother said.

"No, Ma, I rolled them in manure and let 'em dry," he kidded.

"She won't accept he's not the baby anymore," Mr. Hewlitt confided to Chrissa as he passed the platter of steaming corn.

"I can accept he's not the baby, but I can't accept that he doesn't wash before he eats," Thad's mother declared. "I don't want germs sitting at my table."

Thad and Chrissa exchanged smiles.

"You remember that *Far Side* cartoon?" Roger said. "Shows a man coming out a men's room into the restaurant, and everyone's looking his way, because a bell's going off just above the door of the men's room and a neon sign's blinking, 'Did not wash hands.'"

The whole table rocked with laughter. Chrissa loved the laughter—the sheer volume of it.

"You *really* want to work, you should come by the end of September, the apples ready to be shipped to market, the rest to be canned or made into pies," Mrs. Hewlitt said. "You come by any weekend in September or October, and I guarantee I'm up to my elbows in applesauce."

"She is, too!" Thad said, grinning.

"I'll help," said Chrissa.

"Bless you," Mrs. Hewlitt said.

It was a new experience being needed. *Really* needed. Gram seemed to be right about Nick, however. Not once did they mention Chrissa's father. Her mother, either, for that matter. But no one bothered her about the cap.

"I've known Elvina for a long, long time. Pa Jennings and Dad and I used to go hunting together," Mr. Hewlitt told her.

81

Chrissa saw her chance. "What kind of a gun did Gramps have?" she asked.

"What kind of gun? Well, now, I'd have to think about that. . . ."

"Was it a handgun?"

Thad and Roger broke into laughter.

"Now you boys shush," said Mr. Hewlitt. "I've known hunters to carry one so's if the animal doesn't die right off, they finish him with a handgun. Pa Jennings used a rifle. Don't think he carried a handgun, but he was a decent sportsman, I'll tell you that."

There was more talk and kidding, more stories about things that had happened three or four years ago, and when Roger mentioned Thad and Maisie going somewhere together, Chrissa wasn't surprised. Anyone as good-looking as Thad would have a girlfriend already. She was just happy that he let her be a part of his family, the way she was now.

After lunch Mrs. Hewlitt let her go to the orchard with the men. It was the first time she had ever picked peaches off a tree, the first time she had climbed a tree ladder. She panicked halfway up, but looked down into Thad's laughing face.

"Go on, kid. You can do it!" he said.

"Okay, farm-boy, I will," she told him. And she did.

Thad remembered to keep Midnight away from her—gave a low whistle whenever the dog got too close. She stayed the afternoon, long after her legs told her she was tired. Carried the tapered ladder from tree to tree, helped carry boxes to the truck, wanting to do everything that Thad and his brother did, and went home at five only because it was her evening to cook. The Hewlitts insisted on paying her.

"Want me to send Midnight along to keep you company?" Thad joked.

"No, thanks."

"If you'll just pet him once, Chrissa, he'll know you're a friend. Won't bark the next time you come over."

Timorously Chrissa put out her hand and held it there. The dog backed off momentarily, then stretched his head forward, sniffing her hand. He stood still and let her pet him, rewarding her with a lick.

"What was *that* for?" she asked, startled.

"Means you're blood brothers—sealed with a kiss. Lucky dog."

She grinned at Thad. "So long, Midnight," she said, and started home.

As she went back through the woods, the elation of the day gave way to prickles of discontent. *Why* couldn't she have grown up here instead of New York City, where there was always, day and night, a din outside the window and you couldn't see the stars? All this time Chrissa could have been doing what the Hewlitts did—walking in the woods by herself, climbing a tree, carrying a ladder, picking apples.

She banged into the house and clanked a pan onto the stove, oblivious to Gram, who was in the next room massaging one foot. More banging and clattering. Chrissa bumped her leg on an open drawer and kicked it shut. Hard.

"Chrissa, could we have a little less noise, please?" Gram called out to her finally.

She stopped banging then, but nobody could stop her from being angry.

"Ready," she said at last, without expression, and Gram came in from the other room.

When three or four minutes of silence had gone by,

however, Gram said, "Chrissa, what in creation's the matter with you? You have a bad day, or what?"

"No. I had a wonderful day. I've just had a taste of all the wonderful days I've missed in my life, that's what."

Gram put down her fork. "Well, now, if you aren't something! You're the only person I know who can find fault with a wonderful day because her yesterdays didn't measure up."

"Oh, Gram," Chrissa said, letting her shoulders slump. "Things could have been so much better."

"They could have been a whole lot worse."

It was a quiet meal. If only she could have one more chance with her dad, Chrissa thought. If only he had seen the way she climbed those trees, carried that ladder. She *wasn't* the crybaby kid he'd left three years ago, but how would she ever tell him now?

"Gram, I was in the woods the other day and ran into Sister Harmony," she said at last.

"In my woods?"

"Her and that piano player. They told me you were going to give them the woods in your will."

Gram jabbed at her meat. "I don't see that it's any of your business, Chrissa. I really don't."

"But if anyone should inherit it, wouldn't it be Dad?"

Gram didn't even look up. "As I said, it's my business."

Chrissa studied her grandmother. She seemed smaller, somehow. Thinner. And for the first time Chrissa could remember, the old woman ate only half her dinner, then went into the other room to lie down.

◆ ◆ ◆

On Christmas Eve she waited by the window far into the night,

84

because he sometimes got in late from traveling. She didn't know what time it was when she saw her mother standing at the door of her bedroom in her pajamas, a drawn look on her face.

"He's not coming, is he?" Chrissa asked, in a voice so small and strained she could scarcely believe it was hers.

Her mother came over and curled up on the bed beside her, resting her body on one elbow. Chrissa stared at her mother's bare feet as she waited for the answer, at the red polish that was worn off at the ends of the toenails.

"I don't think so," her mother said.

Chrissa rose to a sitting position. "WHY? WHY isn't he coming? What's happened?"

"Nick and I aren't going to live together anymore, honey."

"But WHY?" She was crying now.

"If I knew all the whys, I'd be a wise woman."

Chrissa felt she couldn't breathe, that something was pressing on her chest. How could she face the fact that there would be no more trips to Coney Island with her father again ever? No chance to ride the roller coaster and redeem herself? That he would never come through the door on Christmas Eve carrying a huge stuffed animal under one arm and some store-wrapped presents under the other? Never take her to the playground again and swing her higher than other fathers dared—so high, in fact, that she cried once to make him stop. Now she'd lost her chance to show her spunk. And that's when the sadness moved in and set up house.

◆ ◆ ◆

A letter arrived from the Vital Records section on Monday. Chrissa found it waiting:

Dear Ms. Jennings:
    Regarding your inquiry, the cost of a records search is

twenty dollars, payable by check or money order to the above address. Please fill out the enclosed form and return it with your remittance. . . .

How did she go about sending a check when she had no checkbook? How could she go somewhere to send a money order when Gram would have to drive her?

She wrote to Vital Records again, telling them she would have to trust them with her money. Then she filled out the form, giving her father's full name, took the money Mrs. Hewlitt had given her, and enclosed it with the note. She put it in the mailbox at the end of the drive.

As she started back toward the house, she saw a white Buick coming slowly down the highway. She turned, her body following the direction of the car, until Sister Harmony's Buick came to a stop on the other side of the road.

The piano player was alone. He was wearing dark glasses this time, but Chrissa knew it was him. He merely sat across the road from her, hands on the steering wheel, looking her way, and neither spoke nor smiled.

Swallowing, Chrissa turned toward the house again and quickly walked up the drive.

For the next few weeks Chrissa went every other day to the Hewlitts'. Each time she looked forward to it, and came home bone tired but happy. Most days she was in the kitchen and didn't see much of Thad, but lunchtime was always an occasion, and that alone made the work worthwhile.

Chrissa couldn't tell if Thad looked upon her as a kid sister or someone he liked more than that. He never called her at home, but his eyes lit up when he saw her.

So this is what a family is, she thought once, watching Thad and Roger argue amicably with their father. You can say what you like; you don't always feel you're walking on eggshells. Since most of her memories of her own father had an element of hurt or humiliation in them, why did she pine after him the way she did? It was a puzzle.

She mentioned her reservations about Sister Harmony to Mrs. Hewlitt once, and found a sympathetic ear but no solution.

"I'm not one to repeat gossip, Chrissa, but you wouldn't find me contributing one cent to that woman," Mrs. Hewlitt said. "No, I'll give to my own church, thank you very much. Seems she preaches all over the state—here today, gone tomorrow. The thing I'm thinking is, if she's a true woman of God, why isn't she holding her services in a church? Every preacher has to start somewhere, I know, but churches rent out their rooms to small congregations all the time. Why is it you find her and that nephew of hers in tents, dance halls, and such? It does make you wonder."

"That's why she wants Gram's woods, she says. To build her own church."

"Well, just between us, Chrissa, the Whole Body Church is the last thing I want sitting between your grandma's place and ours, but I've known Ma Jennings long enough to realize that the surest way to get her to do something is to tell her why she shouldn't. One of the liveliest women I know, and also the stubbornest, that's the truth."

Just before Labor Day, Chrissa found a letter waiting from the Vital Records section, and she quickly slid one finger under the flap of the envelope. A form letter inside said, simply, that there was no certificate of death on file for a Nicholas Paul Jennings.

Chrissa stared down at the letter. She began to nourish the hope that her dad was alive after all, but she didn't feel elated, and struggled to understand the heaviness in her chest.

For one thing, he could have died somewhere else. That was reason enough not to hope. But there was something else: If he was dead, he could not possibly have written or called her. But if he was alive, he simply had never bothered. As though he had erased her completely from memory.

12

It was the first Sunday in September, just after lunch, when Sister Harmony paid a call. Gram had not been home from service more than forty minutes when the big white Buick turned up the drive, gravel hitting against its undercarriage as it came.

"Well, look what the wind's blown in," Chrissa breathed, looking out through the curtains.

"Wonder if she's had lunch," was Gram's only comment, and she went outside to welcome her visitor.

They walked about the yard, Gram in her Sunday dress with her Dr. Scholl's sandals taking the place of her oxfords, and Sister Harmony, as usual, all in white. Gram was so eager to show off her mums that she walked bent over, ready to swoop down at a moment's notice to tilt a flower directly into Sister Harmony's line of vision. Chrissa watched helplessly from the window.

For a long time, it seemed, the two women stood by the pond talking, Sister Harmony speaking with dramatic gestures, reaching over now and then to touch Gram on the arm, and Gram listening, her face reflecting all that her ears and eyes took in—shaking her head, pursing her lips, smiling, frowning . . . Finally they started toward the house.

Chrissa began clearing away the luncheon dishes, hoping the women would walk on by her into the living room, but Gram said, "Pour Sister Harmony a glass of iced tea, will you, Chrissa-girl, while I get my checkbook?"

"Now, that will be nice!" the preacher said, sitting down on a chair. "You sugar your tea while it's hot, don't you, Elvina? Makes all the difference in the world."

Wordlessly Chrissa took a jar from the refrigerator and poured some into a glass, ignoring the fact that Sister Harmony's smile was creeping across the table, trying to crawl up under her eyelids. Was it only her imagination, or was there a hint of reluctance in Gram's manner today?

"I think you would have enjoyed the service this morning, Chrissa," Sister Harmony said. "Some lively singing, I'll tell you."

"I enjoyed myself fine staying home," said Chrissa.

Without raising her eyes, she could see Sister Harmony slowly shaking her head. "Still can't control that tongue of yours, can you?"

"I'm controlling it very well," Chrissa said sharply. "Not saying half of what it could."

"That right, now?"

Chrissa looked her straight in the eyes: "I think you're taking advantage of Gram." Did she only imagine it, or did those eyes change color—go from gray to brown to black? It seemed as though all the light had gone out of them, and they were recessing deeper and deeper into shadow.

"Your grandmother has always been a generous woman, Chrissa and she'll— Ah, yes, Elvina, we were talking about that generous soul of yours." Sister Harmony's voice went up a few notes as Gram came back into the kitchen and sat

90

down at the table with her pen and checkbook.

Chrissa leaned against the sink, facing the table. How to stop this?

"Gram!" she said in alarm.

Her grandmother didn't even look up. "It's okay," she said, and Chrissa saw that she was writing a check for two hundred dollars. Sister Harmony's smile spread around the room like honey.

Chrissa stood on the side of the highway in a light drizzle, wearing her fisherman's cap, and watched the yellow bus dip and rise, dip and rise, as it came slowly toward her, pushing its reflection out ahead of it on the glistening pavement.

She had gone to the bus stop early, hoping Thad was there. He was, but so was another boy from across the road, and they were having an animated argument over the New York Giants. Thad merely waved at her with one hand.

Chrissa stood awkwardly to one side, disappointed that she had to share Thad with anyone. Even though he had a girlfriend, she wanted him to like her. Maybe she really *was* too citified for him. Too much like her mother. Not enough of that adventurous spirit her father seemed to have.

She tilted her face up toward the gray-white of the sky as the bus came down the last stretch of road, and let the rain lightly bathe her face. *I want to be like rain,* she thought again. Accepted just as she was.

As the bus veered over toward the shoulder, slowing, she wondered which it was—middle school or high. The driver, a small man in a light windbreaker, looked down at her through the open door, and at that moment Chrissa felt Thad's hand on her arm as he guided her up the steps.

"Charlie always gets here first," he explained to Chrissa. "How you doin', Charlie?"

"How are you, Thad?" the man said, smiling.

And as Chrissa climbed onto the bus, Thad called, "You look out for Chrissa Jennings, now. Treat her right."

The driver smiled. "You Ma Jennings' granddaughter?" he asked as the door swung closed behind her.

Chrissa nodded.

"Glad to meet you." The bus moved on, and Chrissa could see Thad grinning at her through a side window.

That helped. And because she was still smiling at Thad, several people on the bus returned her smile. She tried not to worry about whether or not they would like her. *I'm the rain,* she told herself. She just *was.*

"I like your cap," a girl told her.

"Thanks," Chrissa said.

Once in the building, Chrissa noticed that there was something different about the schools up here. More order. Less chaos. Less noise. When a teacher said, "Listen up," at least ninety percent of the class paid attention.

The teacher she liked best was Mr. Bedlow, in biology. He sat on one corner of his desk, one foot in its brown loafer swinging back and forth beneath his tan Dockers. And as the class quieted down, he began talking softly, so softly that everyone had to hush to hear.

"People ask me sometimes," he began, "why I teach biology. It all boils down to one simple fact, I think: All life on earth is produced by other existing life. The cells of your body go back to the very first life on Earth. Think about that, class. . . ."

Surprising to Chrissa was that the class did. Seemed to, anyway, for silence was all about her.

"For this semester and next," Mr. Bedlow went on, "we'll be studying the human body, what it means to be alive, the differences between living and nonliving things, between plant and animal cells, and the place of human beings in nature. Because we're all tied together. Think about this: The latest theory is that before the big bang, the universe—the whole universe, class—was packed into a space smaller than a single atomic particle."

Chrissa tried to imagine it—herself, one with the rivers, the rocks, the sun, the rain.

Yes! she thought. *I'm going to like this class!*

As the bus navigated the last long rolling stretch of highway on the trip home, Chrissa saw the bus from high school trailing, so that both buses stopped about the same time, and she and Thad and the boy across the road were standing once more on the shoulder of the highway.

"Chrissa, this is Scott," Thad called, motioning to the heavyset boy with glasses and a Florida State sweatshirt. The thing about sweatshirts, Chrissa had noticed, was that they always seemed to be worn by students somewhere else.

"So how's middle school?" Scott asked. "They still serving that same glop in the cafeteria?"

"Cheeseburgers," Chrissa said.

"Hey, things are looking up!"

Scott waited for a truck to pass, then crossed the road, and Thad walked with Chrissa up the long driveway to Gram's house, leaping up every so often to snatch a leaf from a low-hanging branch.

"How's the pond doing?" he asked.

"Gram loves it—always showing off her goldfish. How's the duck calling?"

He smiled. "When hunting season starts, I'll let you know."

When Thad went home, book bag slung over one shoulder, Chrissa watched him head for her own route through the woods, and smiled. It made the connection between them more definite.

She remembered that she had not checked the mailbox, and retraced her steps, hoping that this time, perhaps, there would be something from her father. There wasn't. The Song of the Empty Mailbox. A wonder some country singer hadn't written it yet.

There was a chill in the air that night, and for the first time since she had arrived, Chrissa welcomed the warmth of her bedroom. Bess and Shadow were both asleep on her spread when she went upstairs, and Chrissa stretched out beside them; didn't even protest when Shadow laid his head against her thigh.

◆ ◆ ◆

After the Christmas that was not Christmas at all—not without her father—Chrissa watched for mail. Mom was taking a computer course and was never home before five. Checking for mail as soon as she was home from school, then, became Chrissa's daily ritual. Surely there would be a package waiting for her in the lobby, delayed in the Christmas rush. She asked the building super about it.

"No, little lady, I would have taken it upstairs and put it by your door if there was," he said. "But I'll keep an eagle eye out for it."

The eagle eye didn't help. There was nothing. Not even a note.

◆ ◆ ◆

Chrissa went to the Hewlitts' only on Saturdays now, but they stretched through September and into October. Sometimes when she came out of the woods on the other side, the whole landscape was covered with fog, fingers of fog grasping at the house up ahead.

The peaches had all been picked and either taken to market or put up into preserves and pies. But there were still apples, and Chrissa liked these most of all, for the scent of applesauce and apple butter, warm and spicy, reached her nostrils before she even stepped inside. The huge round bushel of apples on the back steps waited to be pared and processed. The truck, loaded with boxes of apples, waited for its run into town.

"You want to ride with us?" Thad asked her once. "Dad and Roger and I are taking a load to Rochester."

Chrissa looked at the pickup. "There isn't room."

"You and I will ride in back."

Her first thought was no. She might fall out. She might be thrown if the truck stopped quickly. She might . . .

"Sure," she said.

Seated snugly down among the apples, leaning against the back of the cab, Thad beside her, heady with the scent of Staymans, she watched the road unwind behind them.

Now and then they passed stands selling homemade vinegar, sweet cider, and vegetables. Even a green road sign with nothing on it but a bunch of grapes and the word WINERY. If her dad could see her now . . .

The Hewlitts' truck rumbled on, the woods and fields speeding by on either side of her and Chrissa thought how different she was, or was getting to be, from the girl her father once knew. He would have been so proud of her—the way she could climb trees, explore a woods, ride in an open truck—all these things and more.

She looked over at Thad suddenly and smiled. And Thad, puzzled, smiled back.

"Well, how are you liking school up here?" Gram asked one evening as they did some raking.

"It's okay. I like biology a lot."

"Have you given any thought, Chrissie, to what you want to do after high school?"

"Forest ranger," Chrissa said, and laughed when her grandmother looked at her quizzically. "I really don't know, Gram. Most jobs want you to have a college degree, and how is Mom supposed to pay for that?"

"She started a college fund for you. Got four or five thousand dollars in it," Gram told her.

"You're kidding! Where would she get that kind of money?"

"When she sold Nick's car. And she's been adding to it ever since."

Chrissa stopped raking and stared at her grandmother. *Was* he dead, then? "Why would she sell Dad's car?" she asked, her chest tight.

The old woman appeared suddenly flustered. "Well, maybe that's not how she got the money. I don't know, Chrissa. You'll have to ask her. But I do know she's been putting money away for you."

Give Gram enough time and she'd spill the whole thing, Chrissa thought. The problem was, if her father *was* alive, there might not be time enough to find him. Gram did not seem well, and was clearly troubled about something. She used to relax when she got home from her endless care-taker jobs—sit out on the swing with her glass of iced tea, or listen to the classic oldies on WKLX which usually drove Chrissa out to the swing.

But now she was on the phone a good share of the time with Sister Harmony, and it seemed Sister Harmony was doing most of the talking. Gram just listened, her brow furrowed.

"Well, I'll have to think about it," she'd say, and seemed to feel no better after she'd hung up. Chrissa hated to see her grandmother so listless and worried.

She started a little campaign of her own. Whenever Sister Harmony called and Gram was anywhere outside, Chrissa would tell the preacher that her grandmother was unavailable. And then, when Sister Harmony asked that Gram return her call, Chrissa conveniently forgot to tell her.

Gram was out looking at the goldfish one evening when the phone rang at its usual time.

"I'm sorry," Chrissa told the preacher, in her crisp, secretarial voice. "She's unavailable right now."

There was a long pause. Then: "Wherever she is, my girl, you get her. I want to talk to Elvina *now*!"

"I *beg* your pardon?" said Chrissa, using all the courage she could muster.

"Your grandmother's there, and I want to talk to her!"

"I'll tell her you called," Chrissa said, and hung up.

If only she could reach her father. Dad would know what to do about a woman like Sister Harmony.

Then she had another thought: What if her father was right under her nose and she didn't know it? Start with the obvious, she told herself. She picked up the large phone book for the greater Rochester area and looked up Jennings. There was Gram's number, under Elvina. She moved her finger down the list. And there, near the bottom, was JENNINGS, N.

For the next few days, Chrissa dialed the number repeatedly, whenever she had the house to herself. It rang and rang, but no one answered.

13

It was the second week of October. The days were still warm, and with all the windows open, the dry, leaf-scented breeze blew in, fluttering the pages of the wall calendar, sending newspapers scuttling across the floor. If Chrissa sat out too long of an afternoon, however, she needed a jacket. Once, sitting there with her legs drawn up, chin resting on her knees, she heard the faraway sound of Thad Hewlitt's duck call, and found herself smiling.

Gram had taken a Saturday job in Rochester ferrying an elderly woman about on errands, but she got another offer, and came home with a proposition for Chrissa.

"Young widow's rented the old Guilford house up the road," Gram said. "She's working a waitress shift in Rochester on Tuesdays, Thursdays, and weekends, and has two small children to care for. I can do for her during the week, but will recommend you to Mrs. Johnson for the weekends, you want to try it."

"Sure!" Chrissa said, but then she remembered Thad. "What if Mrs. Hewlitt needs me?"

"She needs you bad, I'll sit for you on a Sunday. But this would be steady work, Chrissa. Once the freezing and canning's done, Mrs. Hewlitt won't need you at all."

That was true.

"And anytime you want to invite your young man here, it's fine with me, long as I'm home," Gram added, reading her thoughts.

"Now that's a laugh," said Chrissa. "He's not my 'young man,' Gram. Just a good friend."

Gram's eyes crinkled at the edges. "Sure of that now?"

"Yes. He's *got* a girlfriend. Now, how old are Mrs. Johnson's children?"

"Little girl's four, baby's four, maybe five months. Tiny little thing—premature, I think—but he's getting along. Takes his bottle right down."

"I'll try it."

"Good. Mrs. Hewlitt's given me nothing but praise for you, so I think you'll do fine."

Mrs. Johnson slipped her coat on in the hallway. "I can't let you have friends in, of course. The usual rules. If anyone calls for me, don't say you're here alone."

"Sure," said Chrissa. "It's the same at Gram's."

"And I don't want you to take the children outside."

"Not at all? Even on nice days?"

"Not that many nice days left. Julie has allergies, and being outside wouldn't mean much to Johnny." She smiled. "You'll just have to be creative and do things indoors."

"I'll think of something," Chrissa said, knowing it would be more difficult. She turned back to the children as their mother went out the door.

Could she do this? Chrissa had never sat more than one child at a time, and when she was sitting Bobby Westfall, she knew that Mom was in the apartment above.

She studied little Julie, who had so recently lost her father, and wondered if Mr. Johnson had lived long enough to see the baby at all. Perhaps it was a blessing that the baby had not known him.

"What shall we do first?" she asked brightly. "A book?"

Julie stood leaning against the table, chin tucked under, holding a piece of toast. Her brown hair seemed all the darker against the pale translucent skin of her temples.

"Build something with blocks?" Chrissa suggested. "A tower, maybe?"

Julie's mouth sagged at the corners, tears just out of sight.

Chrissa's eye fell on the rubber doll in the corner, as large as Johnny and almost lifelike. "Feed Baby Doll?"

"Her name's not Baby Doll, it's Susie," Julie offered.

"Should we feed Susie, then?"

"Uh-uh." Julie took a bite of toast.

For want of something better, Chrissa took the empty milk carton off the counter, rinsed it, and opened the top wide. Then, with a handful of clothespins from Mrs. Johnson's laundry basket, she began dropping them one at a time into the carton. Didn't Gram used to do that with her?

"*I* can do that!" said Julie suddenly, taking the pins from Chrissa's hands, and was soon lost in the game.

Johnny, in his infant seat on the table, was in serious need of a change, and that accomplished, Chrissa dressed him mistakenly in Susie's playsuit, much to Julie's delight. The small girl shrieked with merriment when she saw her brother in the doll's overalls, and Chrissa discovered she could easily fill up another ten minutes by knowingly

101

doing something wrong just so Julie could set things right again.

It was at story time that afternoon that she realized how fond she already was of the little girl. Engrossed in the book, Julie leaned over to see the pictures better, and rested one small hand on the back of Chrissa's. It was like looking down on her own hand nine years ago.

◆ ◆ ◆

The awful part, the worst part, was that several weeks after her father had left, he'd sent a postcard to Chrissa with a picture of surfers on it, and somehow it had been thrown out. Chrissa hadn't even checked the postmark, couldn't remember where it was from. He often sent postcards when he was away a long time, usually a scene of some kind—a sailboat, a bridge, a tunnel . . .

"Always nice when business takes me where there's water," the card had said. Chrissa couldn't remember the rest, because she hadn't known it was the last one she would get. And no matter how she willed herself to do so, it had slipped off the edge of her mind.

◆ ◆ ◆

Helping out at the Hewlitts' was far easier than caring for two small children for an entire day, Chrissa discovered. It was surprising how much attention Julie required even when she was sitting still. When she was at the table coloring, for instance, she constantly chirped, "See how good I do this, Chrissa? I can stay in the lines, can't I?" and Chrissa would have to respond. And while Johnny was content to lie peacefully for long periods, babbling to himself or examining the toys in his crib, he might be soaking through. She had to check.

The first day, she came home aching all over, and Gram

102

laughed. "There's nothing as tiring as tending children," she said. "I'll take old folks anytime."

"What's worse is that we can't take them outside," Chrissa complained.

"I know," said Gram. "Just make do."

"I'll bet I could tire Julie out in a hurry if I could get her running around in the leaves. I think the mother's overprotective," Chrissa continued.

But Gram was more understanding. "She's afraid she'll lose her children, too. You lose something precious, you're afraid what's coming next. I'm not over Frank's death yet."

"You think about Gramps a lot?"

"I dream about him, and I do love my dreams." Gram smiled a little.

She was in the bathroom when the phone rang that evening, and Chrissa answered. It wasn't Sister Harmony making the call this time, however; it was her nephew.

"Let me speak to your grandmother," he said gruffly.

"She can't come to the phone. I'm sorry," Chrissa told him.

"Don't give me that." His voice was threatening. "Where is she?"

"How rude of you to ask!" Chrissa responded. She could feel her pulse throbbing in her temples. She wouldn't have the nerve to say this face to face.

"Girl, it's time somebody took you in hand."

Chrissa heard Gram's footsteps on the stairs.

"No, thank you," she said loudly, and hung up.

"Who was that, Chrissie?" Gram called.

"Some salesman," Chrissa told her.

Gram grunted. "Aluminum siding?"

"Cemetery plots," Chrissa answered. Well, it *wasn't* all a

103

lie. They were trying to sell Gram a bill of goods, but they couldn't collect until she was in the cemetery. And Chrissa didn't trust them not to hurry it along.

The thing about Mrs. Johnson was that she kept up a constant patter all the while she was getting ready to leave—as though if she didn't fill up the spaces, somebody else might. Rhetorical questions, mostly, such as, "Now, where did I put my sweater?" or "Can you believe that sky?"

The house they were renting was even older than Gram's, and five miles farther out. There was only one upstairs window from which Chrissa could see any other house at all, and the land all around was wooded. Maybe Mrs. Johnson, too, found a kind of peace in being a part of the seasons.

Chrissa's second day went better, only because she knew what to expect. Julie seemed to be in perpetual motion. You could sit her at the table over a cup of milk and crackers, and she would still bounce up and down on her knees, swiveling her small hips from side to side with some internal rhythm as she chewed.

"Why do you always wear that cap?" she asked Chrissa.

"It belonged to my father," Chrissa told her.

"Oh." Julie was quiet. "*I've* got a cap," she said.

"Want to show it to me?"

"No." She soberly shook her head.

In mid-afternoon Julie was playing with a doll family. She nestled in one corner of the couch, holding the father doll in her hands, crooning a little song and bouncing it on her knee. There was something about the look on her face that made Chrissa say, on a hunch, "Do you miss your daddy?"

At first there was no response. Julie went on bouncing the doll, but stopped humming.

"Was he sick a long time?" Chrissa questioned, thinking perhaps the child would feel better if she talked about it.

Julie shook her head. "Mommy killed him."

Chrissa stared. "Oh, I don't think so."

"Uh-*huh*!"

"Why do you say that, Julie? Why would your mother want to kill him?"

The little girl gave an exaggerated shrug of the shoulders. "He wasn't nice," she said simply.

Chrissa almost had to smile. "How did she kill him?"

"Shot him."

"Really?"

Julie gave her a quick glance as though testing her out, and toyed some more with the father doll, twisting his tie around behind his head. "With a knife."

Chrissa laughed. "She shot him with a knife?"

"A gun, I mean. A great *big* gun." Julie released the father doll and it slid down her leg like a slide. She laughed, picked it up and rolled it some more.

"And then what happened?" asked Chrissa.

The shrug again. "No more daddy!"

"Julie, I think your daddy died because he was sick."

"Lo lah, lo lah, lo lah . . . ," Julie sang, rolling the father doll down her leg, again and again.

The sedate green of the trees became spotted with yellow, then orange, until finally the sky was wearing a collar of crimson. Chrissa left the house a few minutes early each morning just so she could meander through the leaves on the driveway—kicking them out ahead of her, reveling in every breeze that brought a shower down around her shoulders. She thought of sending a box of leaves to her mother, just so Mom could smell that dry fruity scent.

At school she made a friend without trying. Sandy was in several of her classes, including phys ed, and Chrissa realized that the girl often waited for her afterward.

"Ugh! These gym shorts!" said Sandy. "They make me look huge!" The two stood in front of the mirror in the dressing room. "Know what I'm *not* going to be after college, Chrissa? A gym instructor."

Chrissa laughed. "It's the last thing on *my* list."

"What's first?"

"I don't know. Something outdoors, maybe."

That afternoon Thad's bus arrived just behind hers, and Chrissa said, "Guess what? I'll walk you home."

Thad laughed. "Is that a threat?"

"I just want to walk in the leaves." She started back down the highway ahead of him, and Thad followed, chuckling, and occasionally aimed a black walnut at her sneakers. After a while he came up beside her, and the rhythmical *swish, swish,* of the leaves as they walked sounded, Chrissa thought, like the sea.

"Dad always wanted to live by the ocean," she said, and realized she had broached the forbidden subject.

"Who wouldn't?" he replied, and demonstrated how he could hit a road sign twenty yards off with a walnut.

Gram was right; the subject was taboo. Chrissa thought back to all the conversations in the Hewlitt kitchen, and realized that not once had anyone asked about her parents.

She and Thad talked a while at his mailbox, and after he went up the lane, Chrissa sauntered back along the shoulder the way they had come, arms hugging her books to her

106

chest. She walked with her eyes down, feet moving in slow motion. There were too many pieces of the puzzle she didn't have yet. Too many subjects she couldn't discuss. Too many secrets. How she hated secrets!

She was aware of a car approaching ahead of her. The engine grew louder and louder, as though the driver was picking up speed. Chrissa looked up to see a white car racing along the other side of the road, and then, inexplicably, it crossed the center line heading directly for her, but swerved back in time and barreled on.

It all happened too fast for even a scream. Chrissa had thrown herself to one side and lay on the leaves, staring after the car, chest heaving in terror. The face behind the windshield had been unmistakable, however.

The piano player.

14

"He almost killed me."

Those were the first words out of Chrissa's mouth when Gram came home that evening.

Gram paused, coat half off her shoulders. She looked tired, irritable. "Who? What are you talking about?"

"Sister Harmony's nephew! I was walking along the edge of the road after school and he came right at me in their car. I was sure he was going to run me over."

Gram stared at her. "How do you know it was him?"

"I *saw* him, Gram!"

"Didn't he stop? Did he say anything?"

"Gram, he was going seventy miles an hour! No, he didn't stop!"

Gram frowned. "What were you doing along the road?"

"Walking back from Thad's."

"Well, stay off the highway, Chrissa. You shouldn't be walking out there."

Chrissa was exasperated. "Gram, is that all you can say? He almost *killed* me!"

"I'll talk to him, Chrissa, for heaven's sake! I'm sure he didn't mean it. If he didn't stop, he probably didn't even see you. But meanwhile, stay off the road. I've problems enough without that."

Chrissa sat down on one of the kitchen chairs, hands in her lap, and studied her grandmother. This wasn't like her.

"What problems, Gram?"

Gram sorted through the mail there on the table. "They say God doesn't give us any problem we can't handle," she said in reply, "but he's surely testing me."

Chrissa waited. "Anything I can do?" she asked softly.

Gram grunted. "Yes. Keep off the highway."

She *must* be sick, Chrissa thought. Maybe she has cancer or something.

"I'll cook. Go put your feet up," Chrissa told her.

"Now, *that's* a blessing," Gram said gratefully, and went into the next room to take off her shoes.

Sister Harmony called within the hour to tell Gram that her nephew said he'd almost collided with Chrissa on the highway, and didn't she realize that was dangerous? He was so shaken, he hadn't even stopped.

Chrissa listened wordlessly to the explanation and made no comment. The man was lying. He had purposely tried to frighten her. He and his aunt had never wanted her to come, And now that she was here, they did not want her to stay. If she *was* to stay, she had better not interfere with Gram's generosity. That was the message.

"They told me at church last Sunday that whenever you answer the phone, you tell them I'm not available," Gram said, looking at her questioningly.

Chrissa shrugged. "If you were, I wouldn't be answering, would I? I don't see any point in dragging you out of the tub or across the yard unless it's an emergency."

"Well, these knees of mine just don't go as fast as they

used to," Gram said, and let the matter drop.

That evening, when Gram was washing her hair, leaning over the kitchen sink the way she did, Chrissa dialed the Rochester number of N. Jennings once again. It rang three times and Chrissa was counting the rings, ready to hang up after eight, when suddenly a woman's voice said, "Hello?"

"Hello." Chrissa didn't know what to say next.

"Who is this?"

"Chrissa. I was wondering if I could speak to Nick."

"You must have the wrong number."

"Isn't this the home of Nick Jennings?"

"No, it's Noreen Jennings. There's no Nick here."

"I'm sorry," Chrissa said.

Another dead end. It was beginning to seem hopeless.

The weather could not decide between fall and winter. Just when Chrissa thought the cold was there to stay, the sun smiled down and people called it Indian summer. Mice crept into the walls, and she could hear them making their nests. Gram assured her they never came into rooms with cats about, and Chrissa was grateful for Shadow and Bess.

She still spent long stretches of time on the swing by the pond, bundled up in her pea coat, and one evening about dusk she was aware of a sudden commotion in the air, as though a distant audience had just broken into applause.

Looking up, she saw that the trees were filled with starlings. She had never seen so many at once. The sycamore looked as though it had leaves again, fluttering clumps of darkness against the sky. The chirping was raucous and wild. And then, as if someone pressed a button, all noise ceased for a minute or so, before it began again. Eerie.

Later, inside, she worked on her first term paper for Mr.

Bedlow. "Dead or Alive, Plant or Animal?" he had titled his assignment—an essay on things that were hard to classify. Sponges attached to the ocean floor: plant or animal? What was mold? What was mildew?

One of the required texts was *The Lives of a Cell,* by Lewis Thomas. Chrissa sat reading next to the fireplace, Bess snuggled against her, as the burning logs spit and hissed. She absently ran one finger down the cat's spine, and watched the way Bess stretched her body out, extending then contracting her claws in pleasure. Rain pelted down outside, leaving streams that shone silver on the glass:

> ". . . the high probability that we derived, originally, from some single cell, fertilized in a bolt of lightning as the earth cooled. It is from the progeny of this parent cell that we take our looks; we still share genes around, and the resemblance of the enzymes of grasses to those of whales is a family resemblance. . . ."

That's it! Chrissa thought. I *am* the rain. The earth, the grass.

She stared into the flames. The one big change she could see in herself was that she liked herself more. The more she liked herself, the less important it seemed whether or not her father liked her. And yet, she had to find him for Gram's sake. What to try next? Where could she turn?

There was a thunderstorm at Mrs. Johnson's on Saturday, unusual for the end of October. Chrissa had just fed Johnny a perfectly disgusting lunch of strained spinach and squash when she became conscious of how dark the kitchen was getting. Julie noticed too. She stopped her

111

coloring at the end of the table and came to stand next to Chrissa's leg.

"I don't like when it thunders," said Julie.

"Well, it can be pretty loud," Chrissa said.

Outside, the wind picked up. Chrissa could see the tree branches tossing in anticipation.

A flash of lightning. Then KA-BOOM! Julie yelped.

"Tell you what," said Chrissa. "Here's what I used to do when *I* got scared." She rummaged in the cupboard for two pan lids and held them like cymbals. "Sit right here and watch the window, Julie. Every time you see lightning, bang the lids together three times like this."

CLANK! CLANK! CLANK! She demonstrated.

The small girl sat with her legs sticking straight out in front of her.

"There's the lightning, Julie!" said Chrissa.

Eyes wide, Julie brought the pan lids together. CLANK! CLANK! CLANK! CLANK! She blinked every time she banged them, drowning out the thunder that followed.

"See?" said Chrissa. "We're just scaring that old thunder away. Whenever you see lightning, bang those lids."

It was a raucous fifteen minutes. Johnny began to cry at last, unnerved by the noise, but Julie delighted in meeting the enemy head on and beating it at its own game.

Chrissa couldn't help but wonder where her own father was now and whether it was storming there. Whether he had heard the thunder and remembered another little girl, nine or so years ago, who used to be afraid of it too.

"It's okay to be afraid, Julie," she said suddenly, and wished someone had said that to her when she was four.

Mrs. Johnson came home that afternoon with news that

112

the boiler had broken, and the restaurant would be closed the following day for repair, so Chrissa went to church the next morning with Gram. She went not because she wanted to but because she, like Julie, wanted to meet the enemy head on, to show Sister Harmony and her nephew that she wasn't easily scared. Of course they didn't want her here! Give them another six months and they'd have the family farm!

"Where does Sister Harmony hold her services now?" Chrissa asked.

"The old Silver Supper Club," said Gram. "She's got her a good little crowd coming. Hear she's got an even bigger crowd in Albany. I sure do thank her for the blessings she's sent my way." She sounded a little too brave.

The Silver Supper Club, now defunct, had been in a dark room in the basement of Harbinger's Restaurant. The forty-seven people sitting on folding chairs faced the bar, which was covered with little piles of printed tracts and offertory envelopes. HEALING SUNDAY, read a hand-lettered sign. If Sister Harmony had six congregations and went from one to the other, she could be collecting money each week from as many as three hundred people, Chrissa figured.

The nephew sat on a stool at the far end, and Sister Harmony smiled at the worshippers, waving a hymn sheet.

"Glad to see you, Sister Jennings!" she sang out, and then to Chrissa, "I can see a change in your face, indeed I do! This is a day for celebrating now, isn't it?"

"Could be I used Noxema last night," Chrissa murmured dryly as they sat down on the squeaky chairs. Gram chuckled and gave her a playful poke.

The first hymn was "Revive Us Again," and it was sung

113

with vigor, the little congregation growing stronger with each verse, until they loudly belted out the chorus:

"Hallelujah! Thine the glory;
Hallelujah! Amen!
Hallelujah! Thine the glory;
Revive us again."

After the hymn, the reading, and the prayer, Sister Harmony wasted no time launching into the sermon. Chrissa, however, fixed her eyes steadily on the piano player and didn't look away.

". . . This much, sisters and brothers, I can tell you: when the saved get to Heaven, they'll wish they had given more than they did. . . .

"Every penny you give to the Lord is recorded in his ledger book. He has promised to reward each of us according to our need, so God's blessings will come to all who contribute to his work. Do you give enough to the Lord, my friends? Or do you give grudgingly? . . ."

Chrissa exhaled. It was almost hypnotic.

". . . Many seek to find buried treasure, but God is the only treasure you need. . . ."

Chrissa sensed that the nephew knew she was watching him because he seemed to be avoiding her eyes. All during the sermon he leafed idly through the hymn sheets, then got out a small nail file and discreetly filed his nails. Chrissa knew she was getting under his skin when he turned suddenly and stared at her with cold malevolence, and she returned it measure for measure.

The sermon couldn't have lasted more than fifteen minutes, because the congregation was impatient for the

114

healing to begin. The offertory plate went around and Chrissa held it while Gram put in a five dollar bill.

While the nephew played softly, various people came forward. Healing seemed to consist of Sister Harmony placing her fingers around the afflicted part, or close to it—a knee, a shoulder, a back, a forehead—and pressing hard, hard enough to make a person wince. Chrissa could see the preacher's knuckles go white with the pressure.

All the while Sister Harmony's face was tilted up toward the ceiling as she repeated a string of syllables sounding like a foreign chant. When she let go at last, she released the worshipper with a single, swift motion and the order to "Feel God's power! Feel God's love!" And the people returned to their seats smiling, some weeping. "Praise Jesus," they said. "Sweet Jesus! Praise the Lord!"

Chrissa really wondered, when Gram went up to have her knee prayed over, if some miracle had occurred, for, when she returned, she walked with such ease that it seemed amazing. As they left the room at the end of the service, however, Chrissa noticed that Gram once again grabbed the banister and winced with every step.

"Well, what did you think of her today?" Gram asked as they left the parking lot.

"Does she ever preach about anything except money?"

"She's preaching God's word, Chrissa; you're just not listening," Gram told her.

Chrissa stole a look at her. Gram's face was so lined, so *thin,* that Chrissa felt a jolt in her stomach. It wasn't just Gram's knees. She must have some incurable illness, and Sister Harmony knew it. Gram would be leaving her property far sooner than anyone expected, and Sister Harmony and her nephew, like vultures, were circling overhead.

115

15

The first Sunday in November, Gram took care of Julie and Johnny so that Chrissa could help put up the last of the tomatoes at the Hewlitts'. For the first time, Chrissa left her father's cap at home. When she realized it, she was tempted to go back, but didn't. Turned up her collar instead. When she arrived, however, hoping to see Thad, she found that he had gone goose hunting before dawn.

"Where do they go to shoot?"

"There's a marsh they've been going to for the last several years. Nothing we like better than a goose with bacon strips draped over it, cooked on the charcoal grill."

Chrissa worked at slipping off the skins as Mrs. Hewlitt took the tomatoes out of boiling water and passed them over. "Do you ever go with them?" she asked.

Mrs. Hewlitt gave a short grunt. "Get up at two in the morning just so I can sit in a duck blind for six hours?"

"Seems like a lot of work to get a goose," Chrissa said. "Couldn't they just go to the store and buy one?"

The red-haired woman faked a look of shock. "Don't even *mention* it! There's something about going after your meal, shooting it, and bringing it home that makes the meat a little sweeter. So they say. It's a male thing, Chrissa. I don't understand it; I just cook it."

It was ten when the mud-splattered pickup came rolling up the drive. Midnight leaped over the side, his coat still damp, as Chrissa threw on her jacket and went out.

"Four!" Thad called to his mother as she came to the door. "Dad and I each got one, and Roger got two!"

"Looks like we'll be having goose for Thanksgiving!" Mrs. Hewlitt said.

"Want to take one home, Chrissa?" Mr. Hewlitt called.

She laughingly recoiled. "Not on your life."

It was a new experience, being a part of this "male thing." Chrissa sat on the back steps, watching as Thad and Roger and their father pulled off their muddy boots, their bounty laid out on newspapers on the grass. Mrs. Hewlitt brought a pail of boiling water, and each goose was plunged into the water, then laid across one of the hunter's knees.

"Hmmm, good!" Roger joked. "Essence of goose."

To Chrissa it was one of the worst things she'd ever smelled—the dank, acrid odor of wet feathers. It made her turn her face away and suck fresh air into her nostrils.

She studied the goose on Thad's lap as he sat there in his stocking feet, methodically plucking the feathers. The broad white band across its throat and cheeks was stained with blood, the eyes opaque.

"Do you ever feel—well, the least bit guilty about killing one?" she asked.

"Nope." Thad held the skin taut with one hand while he plucked with the other. "It's all a matter of balance. If nobody shot any, the goose population would get out of control. Shoot too many, and they'll go somewhere else. You've got to eat them and protect them, both."

117

Chrissa thought it over as she patted the Labrador. Hadn't even known she was doing it until she looked down and saw her hand resting on his head. He looked up at her gratefully, eyes closing from time to time in weariness.

"What happened after you fired the guns? I mean, what did the other geese do? Scatter?"

"No, just kept on."

Strangely, she felt a part of all this—the cycles, the seasons, life and death, birth and destruction, the kill, the feast—and was encouraged by it. Encouraged by the flight of the geese when the killing was over. Strengthened to know that the flock could carry on.

The phone rarely rang in the evenings anymore. Now that Chrissa was working weekends, Sister Harmony paid her visits then, and Chrissa wondered if she had helped Gram at all by deflecting her phone calls; it was probably easier for Gram to refuse over the phone than it was in person, and Chrissa was no longer around to stand guard.

She had already finished her first biology paper and had started the second, "Regenerating Yourself," about the body's constant manufacture of blood cells, skin cells, hair, fingernails. *Born again,* Sister Harmony would probably call it, but regeneration had a different meaning for Chrissa. It meant a new chance every day, not a once-in-a-lifetime event.

She liked the idea that she, like trees shaking off leaves in the fall and growing buds in the spring, was also a cycle of sorts. That there was a dependable ebb and flow to her life. Back in the city, her life had been governed by whether she was in or out of school. Up here she was more attuned to the seasons, the wind, the trees, and the geese that would, come spring, fly north again.

It was a problem trying to keep up with homework and housework, too, and with the holidays approaching, Gram wanted the house cleaned thoroughly.

"It's only you and me," Chrissa reminded her, but Gram was adamant.

So Chrissa was dusting one evening, taking her time with Gram's owl figurines, when she bent down to pick up the old family Bible from the lower shelf of the end table. And it was then she discovered the letter.

Written on a sheet of notepaper and folded in thirds, it had obviously been used as a bookmark. Heart thumping, Chrissa glanced into the kitchen where Gram was scraping the bottom of the skillet, then sat down on the sofa and unfolded the letter. She knew immediately that it was her father's handwriting. No address, no date:

Mom—

Got your letter, and don't know what to advise about that certificate. Might be you could get a higher interest rate somewhere else. Call some S&Ls and see how they measure up.

Been putting on a few pounds. Not enough exercise. Need some dental work, too. Fellow here in Watertown owns a little boat-building company. Not a whole lot of work around here, but I'm thinking he may take me on in the business somewhere down the road.

Figure Chrissa's doing okay, you didn't say. You have any photos of her, send me one.

Nick

Alive! Her father was alive and asking about her! Chrissa sat with one hand over her mouth, eyes wide.

She knew the name of the town now, and nothing, *nothing,* would keep her from finding his address. Exactly the kind of place she imagined her father would be. Precisely the kind of work he might be looking for. But what state? Watertown what?

Think, she told herself, putting the letter back exactly as she'd found it. Her head felt giddy. Dad had always wanted to live on the coast, and he mentioned a boat-building business. She would check a map at school and go right down the coast till she found it.

She went to the school library the next day after lunch and picked up the atlas by the window. Tense with excitement, she carried it to a chair in one corner. Each state was given its own map and, on the back, the list and locations of all its cities and towns. Chrissa started with Maine. Waterville, but no Watertown.

She moved on down the coast to a little piece of New Hampshire, then found the list of cities for that. No Watertown. On to Massachusetts. And there it was: D-2. Bingo! Turning the page over to the map, she put her finger on it—a small dot on a river just outside Boston.

How could it be this easy? But there it was, Watertown, Massachusetts, and the little dot seemed almost to jump before her eyes.

Chrissa let out her breath. How could she find out when Gram had received that letter, and whether her father was still there?

"Thad," she said that evening as they walked up the drive after school, before he took his usual route through the woods. "How would you go about finding a friend who moved around a lot? Always on the road, I mean."

"You know the last address?"

"The town, but no street number."

"Well, start with the phone. See if the operator has a listing for her parents. It's a girl, I guess?" He looked at her sideways, and when she didn't answer, he said "Okay, a *guy*, huh?"

"Just a friend," said Chrissa.

"Well, if he's not listed, send a letter general delivery. They'll hold it at the post office a certain number of weeks. People who don't have a fixed address just go to the post office every few days and ask if they have any mail, general delivery. That's the way we stayed in touch with Roger when he hitchhiked to California one summer. He gave us his route, and Mom would write ahead to the next town, general delivery."

"That's all I have to do?"

"You were expecting a page of instructions?"

She laughed.

It was just before study hall the next day that Chrissa went to the pay phones outside the cafeteria.

"What city, please?"

"Watertown, Massachusetts."

"Yes?"

"Do you have a listing for Nicholas P. Jennings?"

"One moment."

Chrissa had never thought of herself as nervous, but suddenly the wait seemed unbearable. Dry mouth. Lump in the throat. Sweaty palms.

"I'm sorry, there is no listing for Nicholas P. Jennings."

Disappointment, sharper than Chrissa expected, stabbed at her stomach.

"Would you have a Nick Jennings? N. Jennings?" she asked.

"No, neither Nicholas, Nick, or N."

Chrissa put down the receiver and stood for a long time with one hand on the phone. Then she had a another thought.

Unlisted! She hadn't considered that. He didn't want Mom to bug him. "He's there!" she whispered. She could feel it. She'd find him yet.

Mr. Nicholas P. Jennings, Chrissa wrote on the envelope. *General Delivery, Watertown, MA.* Just in case her father *didn't* have a fixed address, she was taking Thad's advice. She hastily checked over the letter again:

Dear Dad,

You probably know I'm spending the year at Gram's and going to school here. I like it. It's different anyway.

If you've been writing, I haven't been getting your letters. I'm working weekends taking care of two little kids at the old Guilford place, as Gram calls it, and learning to do a lot of things I couldn't do before.

I really need to talk with you. I don't know how you feel about seeing me, but I don't think Gram is well. She's made friends with a preacher here, and is planning to give her the woods to build a church. I think Sister Harmony and her nephew are taking advantage of Gram. You wouldn't like them, I'm sure of it.

Please call Gram. She needs you. Even better, please come.

Chrissa

"What time does the mailman come?" Chrissa asked when she got to Mrs. Johnson's on Saturday. "I forgot to leave this letter at our box." She didn't dare leave it where Gram might find it.

"Don't put it in ours, he'll never take it," Mrs. Johnson said. "I'll mail it for you in town. I keep a box at the post office—don't even bother with rural delivery."

Would she tell Gram that Chrissa had posted a letter to her father? Or would she even know? Chrissa handed the envelope wordlessly to Mrs. Johnson, who didn't bother to look at it—just dropped it in her purse.

16

She missed being at the Hewlitts' on weekends. A second irritation was having to stay inside at Mrs. Johnson's. Sometimes when both children were napping, Chrissa would throw on her jacket and set the phone on the back porch where she could hear it if it rang. Then she would stroll about the yard, hands thrust in the pockets of her pea coat.

Thirty yards to the left of the house, in among the trees, was an old service road, more like a cow path, actually, overgrown with weeds. It paralleled the driveway, and once in a while a car bumped by on it, a neighbor taking a short-cut. Chrissa would have liked to explore it, but of course she would not leave the property.

A cold grayness crept in over the land. The branches of the sycamore looked like claws against the sky, and the air was filled with the death rattle of dry leaves. There were moments Chrissa had the feeling that her father was close by—closer than she'd thought. It might have been some of his mannerisms that she found in Gram—an inflection of voice, perhaps.

"Mrs. Hewlitt told me there's talk of another road being

built here somewhere—everyone's worried it's going to run through their land," Gram told her. "Said she saw surveyors herself the other day, across the highway."

What *was* the resemblance? Chrissa wondered, dismayed that she couldn't put her finger on it. As though she was losing her father—even the memory of him—bit by bit.

"I see any surveyors on *your* property, I'll run them off," Chrissa promised, making Gram laugh. She enjoyed making her laugh now, she laughed so little.

Maybe it was Gram's laugh that sounded most like Dad's. She could not help but think, however, that some morning she was going to come downstairs and find him at the table. Look out the window and see him standing in the grass.

She was thinking again about little Julie. There was something about her play that bothered Chrissa. She liked her blocks, liked her big doll, and enjoyed coloring with Chrissa. But there were times when Julie played with the small father doll that every conceivable thing seemed to happen to him. He fell off the back of the sofa on his head and Julie giggled. The little fire engine ran over his legs and Julie laughed out loud. Towers of blocks fell on him or he was put upside down in a paste jar. Sometimes Julie would take him out and kiss him, then stick him back inside.

"Do you have any idea how Mr. Johnson died?" Chrissa asked Gram as they did the dishes after dinner.

"Car accident, I think she told me."

"How old was Julie then?"

"That one I don't know."

"Have you ever noticed how she plays with that father doll of hers? All sorts of terrible things happen to it."

Gram nodded. "Now that you mention it, I guess I've

seen that, too. They say, you know, that if a child is young when a parent dies, she thinks he left her on purpose. I figure it's normal anger coming out, that's all."

"She says her mother shot him."

Gram paused with the spoons in her hand. "No one can beat that child's imagination! You ask her tomorrow, I'll bet she has a different story."

So the next day, as Chrissa and Julie were eating their afternoon snack, Chrissa said, "I forget, Julie. How did your father die?"

"Drowned," said Julie. "In the lake."

Gram had said once that Chrissa didn't love enough, but she certainly loved this little four-year-old girl who was so needy. In need of all the things that Chrissa had needed at four. Somehow Chrissa would help her through.

The nice thing that was happening, now that she wasn't helping out at the Hewlitts' on weekends, was that Thad started calling her once in a while. It was easy to talk to Thad. Natural. Nice to get to know a guy first as a friend instead of worrying about having or not having a "boyfriend."

One evening Gram was cleaning out her wallet on the dining room table. She spread the contents before her— driver's license, Social Security, credit cards . . . Chrissa, working on her term paper across the table, noticed the photograph of herself taken last year in seventh grade, with the hair that always seemed to stick straight up. The smile was nice though. Mom always sent a strip of school pictures to Gram. So Chrissa asked, "Does Dad know what I look like now?"

"I imagine he does," said Gram.

126

"Do you send him pictures?"

"I've sent one."

"That one?" Chrissa pointed to her seventh-grade photo and waited.

Gram nodded and held it out in front of her. "It's the best one of you, don't you think?"

"Definitely," Chrissa said.

If Gram had sent that photo, taken in May of seventh grade, it was probably in response to his request in the letter Chrissa had found stuck in the Bible. If he was in Watertown as late as last May, he could be there still.

Just when Chrissa began to hope she could find him in time, however, her grandmother dropped the bombshell:

"What I'm thinking of doing, Chrissie—and I'm not asking your advice, I'm telling you—is deeding my woods to the Whole Body Church of the Lord right now, instead of waiting till I'm gone." She ignored Chrissa's gasp and continued: "Now I'd set aside some for you, to help with college, but not a soul on this earth knows when she's going to die, and if I surprise everybody and live to ninety, what good will it do Sister Harmony then? It's *now* she's needing a church. One day she's preaching one place, the next day another. . . . Sundays, she tells me, she's got three different congregations to tend to, all seventy miles apart."

"Gram, you've got to talk to someone about this! You really should," Chrissa said earnestly. "I mean, it's great you want to help me with college and everything, but maybe you should talk to the Hewlitts. Get some advice."

Gram gave her a quick, impatient glance. "I don't go talking over my private business with the neighbors, Chrissa, and I don't expect you to either. What I do with my land is my business."

"Yes, but—"

"Sister Harmony's even promised to name a room in the church for your grandfather. Why that would just please him so!"

"Gram, listen to me!" Chrissa cried. "Yes, it is your land, and it's not the Hewlitts' business, but shouldn't you at least tell them about it in advance so they won't wake up some morning and find a church sitting there?"

Gram chuckled at the thought. "Oh, word will get around before then, you can bet. Soon as I deed those woods over, the folks at the courthouse will talk."

"But you've got to tell Dad!" Chrissa pleaded. "Just promise me that, Gram. Tell Dad what you're planning to do before you sign anything."

In despair Chrissa waited for her grandmother to answer, but the old woman slowly put things back in her wallet without a word.

Next week was Thanksgiving. If ever Dad was going to call Gram, it would be then. Chrissa would answer the phone when it rang, and she'd tell him everything. *Everything!*

Both Chrissa and Gram were invited to the Hewlitts' for Thanksgiving dinner, the main entrée being wild goose.

"I don't believe I've ever tasted meat so sweet," said Gram, holding a wing in her hands and nibbling hungrily.

"Someday we're going to have wild turkey on this table," Mr. Hewlitt announced. "Used to go with my father to bottomland to hunt wild turkeys. You go where there are acorns, and that's where you'll find the turkeys."

"Is there a turkey call?" Chrissa wanted to know.

"Indeed there is, but what you want to do is go at the first light of day. Then you make an owl call. That upsets a turkey. It'll get to gobblin' so's you can find him."

"How do you ever *learn* all this?" Chrissa asked.

"You grow up a Hewlitt," Thad said, and laughed.

Chrissa enjoyed the food and the board games at the table afterward, but she really had wanted to stay home in case her father called.

It was near seven when she and Gram got home, and just as Chrissa expected, the phone was ringing. she bumped her shin trying to get there in time, and was deeply disappointed when she heard her mother's voice.

"Oh, it's you," she said flatly, realizing too late how it sounded.

Mother chose to laugh it off. "Sounds to me as though you were expecting a friend. Would this be a boyfriend, by chance?"

"Something like that," Chrissa told her.

When she finished talking, she went into the living room, where Gram was watching TV and furtively trying to put out the butt of a cigarette in her coffee cup.

"Gotcha!" said Chrissa, as Gram tried to slide the cup behind her foot on the floor.

"Oh, Chrissie, don't ever start. It's the worst habit in the world, and it'll stink up your breath something fierce."

"I've got enough bad habits as it is," Chrissa told her. "Don't need any more."

She sat down beside Gram on the sofa to watch the program, but she was listening for the phone. Surely, wherever he was, Dad would call his mother on Thanksgiving. But seven became eight, and eight became nine. The phone didn't ring again, and Gram went to bed.

November slid into December, icy and cold. Chrissa gave up

wearing her father's Greek sailor cap and chose a wool stocking cap instead. She hated to see the end of autumn but, at the same time, welcomed each change of seasons because it was something she could count on, something sure.

Dear Chrissa:

It seems strange to be thinking of Christmas without you in the house, and I wonder if you might like to come home for the holidays. Gram is invited too, of course.

There have been times, believe it or not, when I wish you were here, silences and all. I know I did and said things I wish I hadn't, but this works both ways.

Perhaps before you come home, we could each make a list of the things that bother us most about the other. Maybe that's how we should begin. . . . Why don't you talk it over with Gram and let me know if you want to come?

Love, Mom

Dear Mom:

I have a lot of assignments piling up over Christmas vacation, so guess I'd better stay here. Got my grades last month—three Bs, a C-, and a B+. I'm doing okay, I guess. Why don't you come here if you don't want to spend Christmas alone?

Chrissa

She should have added more—should have said, *I'd really like you to come.* But even as she thought it, Chrissa's fingers sealed the envelope and put a stamp on the front.

Dear Chrissa:

I can tell you're still angry, so maybe it's better that we spend Christmas apart. I'll find plenty to do here. Will be getting off some presents for you and Gram one of these days. Take care. . . .

                                                            Mom

"Don't be too hard on her, Chrissie. Lorraine hasn't had an easy life," Gram said. "Her father was an alcoholic, you know. She could never invite friends in when she was your age, and even then, he embarrassed her and her sister something awful. Now she's going it alone, and it's hard to be a parent all by yourself."

"Well, I haven't exactly had an easy life either," Chrissa responded, and let it go at that.

At Gram's, Chrissa was beginning to find what she missed in the city—the way things fit together. Everything depending on everything else. The birds she fed in the winter ate the insects that bothered her in June and July. The trees that shaded her in August now stood bare of leaves, allowing the sun to warm the porch in December. Giving and taking. A kind of balance to things.

Chrissa set herself more and more difficult tasks, just to see if she could do them. Carrying Gram's ancient vacuum sweeper upstairs with one hand; bringing in wood for the fireplace in two armloads instead of four; making an obstacle course for herself of logs and tree stumps when she walked through the woods; toughening herself up.

It was almost Christmas, and in return for the Esprit socks and shirts Mom had sent, Chrissa and Gram had packed up six jars of homemade strawberry jam to send to her. A natural exchange.

Chrissa and Gram had let each other select their own presents. Chrissa chose a shirt and some jeans from a catalog, and Gram picked out a fluffy new robe. When Gram opened the box on Christmas morning, however, she found that Chrissa had included a pair of warm slippers to match.

"Now Chrissie!" Gram scolded, obviously pleased. "Where did you get the money to buy all this?"

"I'm a working girl, remember?" Chrissa told her, and was delighted the slippers fit exactly.

Once again, however, Chrissa's father did not call, putting a damper on the holiday spirit, at least for her. If he didn't call his mother at Christmas, he would not call at all, Chrissa decided. She toyed with the idea of asking Gram if she might call him, and finally took the plunge:

"Do you think I could call Dad and wish him merry Christmas?"

And after the question had hung in the air for a moment or two, Gram said, "Did you call him last Christmas?"

"No, I don't know his number."

"Well, neither do I," Gram replied.

She was maddening. If she knew his address, how could she *not* know his phone number?

It was Thad who saved Christmas. He knocked on the door about four that afternoon and presented Chrissa with a present. She stared. "Well . . . gosh, Thad! Thanks!"

"Invite him in, Chrissie, for heaven's sake," called Gram and immediately thrust a saucer of brownies at him.

Embarrassed because she had nothing for him in return, Chrissa fumbled with the ribbon. Out fell two blocks of wood, hinged at one end, one of them hollow. "What *is* it?"

He grinned. "Turkey call—rock maple. One of Dad's."

"What? How do you do it?"

Thad took the blocks in one hand and rubbed them together. They made a strange sort of chirping noise.

"You've got to be real careful to do it soft and not too long, like this," he said, continuing the demonstration. "One sour note, and the turkey's gone."

"What am I supposed to *do* with this?" Chrissa asked.

"In case you ever get hungry for wild turkey," Thad said, and they both had a laugh over that.

He stayed for a half hour, time enough for a second helping of brownies, and after he was gone, Chrissa caught Gram leaning back in her chair with her eyes closed.

She went over and stroked her arm.

"Gram, don't you think you should see a doctor?"

One eye opened, then the other. "What for? What ails this old body, Chrissie, a doctor can't do a thing about. Now don't you spoil your Christmas. Turn up those carols! I can hardly hear them."

What if Gram had only a year or two left? Who would take care of her after Chrissa went back to New York City? Chrissa watched as her grandmother got up later to stir the fire, and ached for the small woman whose shoes always seemed too big for her feet. And for the first time, she wondered if Mom would let her stay another year. Long enough to find Dad and tell him what was going on.

17

Winter closed over the land, as far as Chrissa could see, and still she had no reply from her father. A row of icicles hung from the eaves outside her bedroom window. Sometimes, if the sun was strong, she could hear the *drip, drip* of water from their tips, hitting the ground below, but mostly they hung there from day to day, winter's teeth outside her window.

The pond had long since frozen over. The snow came and stayed, untrampled except for occasional hoofprints of deer, or the pawprints of possum and raccoon, futilely circling the pond.

Once Chrissa tramped over to Thad's after school. She sat in the Hewlitts' kitchen and talked and laughed, kidded around with Thad and enjoyed a dish of applesauce she had helped make, and a molasses cookie baked that morning.

"Tried out that turkey call yet?" Thad asked.

"Not yet." She smiled impishly down at her applesauce. "Did you give Maisie one, too?"

"What?" Thad paused, a cookie halfway to his mouth, and even Mrs. Hewlitt turned around from the stove.

Chrissa shrugged, embarrassed. "Your girlfriend."

"My *girl*friend?" Thad laughed. "Chrissa, Maisie was my *dog*! One of them, anyway."

Chrissa blushed to the roots of her hair, but Mrs. Hewlitt threw back her head in laughter.

Well, what do you know! Chrissa thought. Maybe she was Thad's girlfriend after all. Farm boys sure took their time about things. She sort of liked that.

Chrissa enjoyed the walk back from the Hewlitts', finding herself a target for the huge clumps of snow that fell from the trees whenever a gust of wind penetrated the woods. It was the glistening, however, that she liked most. When the sun shone hard and white on the icy crust over fields and fence posts, a shimmering took place—tinkly sparkles of ice crystals all trembling together, giving off sparks, it seemed. And the quiet! The countryside had been soundproofed with the cold white foam of winter. Everything seemed to be waiting . . . waiting. For spring. For thaw. For life.

Chrissa, however, was waiting for mail. She went through her routine of school assignments, of cooking for Gram and cleaning up, of lunch with a friend or two in the cafeteria, talking with Thad after school. Sometimes Gram drove her to the shopping center and she saw a movie with Sandy. Or she went bowling with Thad and his brother and sister-in-law. She went to Mrs. Johnson's on weekends and put in her stint as a sitter. But her eyes watched the mailbox, and each day the letter she waited for never came.

Dear Mom, she wrote, the third week of January, feeling the need to connect with someone:

It is really beautiful here in the snow; it's almost like another land, so different from N.Y.C. You should be

135

with me sometime when I walk through the woods. No people. No houses. No sounds. It's so quiet you can hear yourself swallow. I'm not kidding.

This will surprise you, I know, but I wonder how you'd feel about me staying at Gram's for another year. I haven't asked her yet, but I think she'd let me. More than that, she needs me. I don't think she's well. . . .

Gram stopped going to Wednesday night services because she didn't like driving through snow in the dark. So Sister Harmony and the piano player came to her. The nephew dropped off the preacher and went on down the road to see some of the other members of the congregation.

Chrissa sat across the room doing her homework while Gram and the woman in white talked together on the couch. Gram held the Bible in her lap, following along as Sister Harmony read the Scripture, then scrunched her eyes tightly shut, chin up, when the praying began.

"It's when things look darkest, Elvina, that God's work is about to begin," the preacher said. "Think of it as an opportunity to show God you love Him, that you can make a commitment as big as the commitment you expect from Him. Don't hold back, if you want Him to come through for you."

Chrissa felt sick inside. Was Sister Harmony asking for the deed to the woods now? She would never be satisfied until she had Gram's house and car as well.

So intent were the two women in their prayers that they didn't hear the doorbell, so Chrissa answered.

The piano player stood there in his overcoat.

"Sister Harmony about ready to go?" Steely eyes fixed on Chrissa, he stepped forward as though intending to enter the kitchen, but Chrissa, blocking the door, didn't budge.

"You want her, I'll get her," she said in reply, but didn't move. Her eyes never left his face, and she amazed herself. Six months ago she could never have done this.

Seeing that he wasn't going to be asked in, the man cocked his head slightly, a smile that was both a beginning and end on his lips. "You think you're really somebody, don't you?"

"I *am* somebody!" Lord, yes.

"You get a little spunky, and you think you've got the bull by the horns, running the show," the piano player said.

His words made her angrier still. "What do you want from Gram, anyway? A human sacrifice?"

It was not a smile on his face. Chrissa had been mistaken. It was a sneer.

"I think your grandmother is old enough to know her own mind," the piano player said.

"She's old and sick, that's what she is, and you're just waiting for a chance to move in," Chrissa said huskily.

"You watch yourself, little girl. You go poking your nose in somebody's business, you may get more trouble than you bargained for. Just watch yourself," the piano player told her.

Chrissa whirled around and marched defiantly into the living room.

"Your ride's here," she said.

The strangest part of all, Chrissa discovered, was that in talking with Sister Harmony's nephew, it was almost as though she were talking to her father, the way he put her down. Talking to him in a way she had never talked before.

Mr. Hewlitt came over after school one Friday with a load

137

of firewood for Gram, Thad sitting in the pickup beside him. Gram was already home, and glad to see them.

"Get your boots on," Thad told Chrissa as he helped stack wood by the back door. "I brought a couple of sleds. We'll try out your driveway. It's ice all the way down."

"I didn't know you had sleds, Thad!"

"We don't get them out very often—our land's too flat. You're the one with the sloping driveway. Let's go."

Chrissa pulled on her boots, put on a pea coat, cap, and mittens, and came out. She tried the smaller of the two sleds, and watched as Thad took a running start, threw the sled down on the ice, his body on top of it, and went careening down the drive.

"I'll break my neck!" Chrissa told him when she saw him coming back up again, walking in the new snow alongside.

"Try it!" Thad laughed, his cheeks red as apples.

Chrissa lumbered through the snow in her heavy coat toward the driveway, broke into a run, and, throwing the sled down ahead of her, tried a belly flop, but the sled streaked out from beneath her and she bumped her chin on the ice.

Thad broke into laughter, but he returned the sled.

"I *told* you I couldn't do it," Chrissa said, struggling to her feet and wiping her mouth.

"Close. Try again." Thad's eyes were laughing still.

She watched as he did it again, then tried to imitate him, and at last made it onto the sled.

"You two going to horse around outside, I'll sit and have a cup of coffee with Elvina," Thad's father called.

Thad waved him on, and went about giving Chrissa another lesson.

"You're getting the hang of it," he told her as they

138

tried again. Three, four, five times they did it.

"I don't even remember being on a sled before," Chrissa confided as they walked back up the drive, he in the snow on one side, she on the other. Between them the ice reflected the late gleam of the sun.

"Never?"

"Where would I go sledding in Chelsea?"

The door opened and Mr. Hewlitt came out again. "I'm going, Thad," he called. "Throw those sleds in the back."

"No, let's leave 'em here for a while," Thad told him. "Go ahead, and I'll walk home later."

Mr. Hewlitt got in the truck, and this time he turned it around in the snow, then started down the driveway.

Thad chuckled and nudged Chrissa. In a flash he belly-flopped on the sled right behind the pickup, reaching up to hold on to the bumper with one hand.

Instantly Chrissa followed. She hit the ground about the same time she heard Thad shout. She felt herself fairly skimming along the ground, a solid layer of ice beneath her.

From down there, the rear of the truck looked higher than she remembered, and as the sled gained speed, she raised one hand to grab the bumper. She remembered only the blur of Thad's face as she passed him—his eyes huge, mouth distorted—and she was under the truck.

A yell from Thad, the thunk of brakes, and suddenly Chrissa was twisting about, exhaust filling her lungs. The next thing she knew she was lying on her side, the shoulder of her coat caught on something above, one of the wheels an inch from her cheek.

Mr. Hewlitt leaped out of the truck.

"Thad! What the blazes—"

"Chrissa!" Thad's voice, husky. "Chrissa, you okay?"

The slam of the back door.

"What's happened?" Gram's voice—tight and high.

Chrissa knew she was unhurt. Nothing had been run over, but the terror of it was a physical thing, like a rock stuck in her throat, huge and painful.

Hands were clasping at her, gently pulling her out, and Chrissa inched herself along on one elbow until she was clear of the truck. Thad's face was white.

"What*ever* possessed you to try something like that?" said Mr. Hewlitt.

"I didn't mean for *you* to do it," Thad said to Chrissa.

"*Both* of you! That's a damn stupid thing to try." said Mr. Hewlitt's face was purple.

Gram was plunging through the snow in her slippers, eyes wild.

"I—I'm okay, Gram," Chrissa said, getting to her feet, her voice a mere whisper. But the old woman grabbed her by the arm and half dragged her toward the house, leaving Thad with the two sleds beside his father.

Somehow Chrissa managed to turn and wave, and then she was in the kitchen and Gram shoved her down on a chair.

"Fool!" Gram was angry, but there were tears in her eyes. "Summer's fool and winter's idiot, I swear to God! Where's your *sense*, Chrissa? Where is your sense? I'm to call Lorraine and tell her your head was crushed out on the driveway?" And suddenly she grabbed Chrissa's head and held it against her. "Oh, Chrissie, if anything happened to *you*, it would be more than a body could bear."

Chrissa welcomed this sudden, desperate hug, the depth of Gram's caring, even though she *had* been humiliated in front of Thad.

"It looked so easy," she said meekly, and realized she was shivering all over. Her teeth chattered with fright.

Gram noticed, too. She dropped her arms and knelt down, pulling off Chrissa's boots, then went into the living room for the afghan and put it over Chrissa's lap. She clanked the teakettle on a burner and lit the fire.

"It's the things that look easy that'll trick you," she murmured, still staring at the wall. She slowly shook her head. "I can remember when I thought that getting married and raising a child were the easiest things in the world. What could be more natural than that? You get to be my age, Chrissa, you'll find that what seems hard now will turn out to be easy when you see what's coming at you down the line."

What was she talking about? Chrissa wondered. Illness? Death? She was too tired to think and, closing her eyes, gave herself to the warmth of the afghan and the hot tea Gram had placed on the table.

Thad called later. "Got chewed up one side of my head and down the other going home," he said. "I don't think I ever saw my dad so angry. You're okay, aren't you?"

"Just shaken up a little," Chrissa told him. "My face was *that close* to a wheel, Thad!"

I know. I didn't realize you'd try it. I'm sorry."

"Well, it was my fault. *I'm* sorry," said Chrissa.

"I'm sorrier." Chrissa heard him laugh. "Listen, how about coming over and playing 'Sorry'?"

Chrissa laughed a little, too. "I doubt Gram will let me out of the house for a while. I'll take a rain check."

At the Johnsons', Chrissa found reasons to praise Julie every chance she got.

"You're the best helper!" she would say as they gathered up the toys. Or, "I love to hear you sing!"

She thought of her praise as salve on a wound.

To while away the long cold weekends indoors, Chrissa had Gram drive her to the library, where she loaded up on picture books for Julie. The little girl's favorites were two wordless books called *Sunshine* and *Moonlight.*

With Johnny lying on his back on the couch, playing with the bracelets on Chrissa's hand, and Julie snuggled against her, Chrissa and Julie would go through those books again and again, soaking up details. What engrossed them was the interaction of the little girl and her father—a kindly-looking man who did not scold when his small daughter climbed on the bed in the morning and woke him up. A father who sat on the floor beside her at night reading a story.

"Some daddies are like this, Julie," Chrissa said. She saw it in Thad's father. She saw it in Mr. Bedlow at school when he talked in class about his children.

Julie sat very quietly looking at the pictures.

"My daddy's dead," she said finally. "He got killed by a train."

Chrissa had received a C+ on her first term paper from Mr. Bedlow and a B on the next, and was already researching "I Owe My Life to Trees." She liked the titles he gave them, this one to focus on the symbiotic relationship between plants and animals.

More often than not, Chrissa did her homework on the bed, papers spread out around her with one or both cats to keep her company. Every so often she paused to look out the low windows at the leafless trees, discovering squirrels' nests that now sat exposed and vulnerable without their protective covering of leaves.

She could tell by the tire tracks in the driveway when Gram had visitors. After Mrs. Johnson drove her home at the end of a Saturday or Sunday, Chrissa often found two sets of tire tracks in the fresh snow, one of them from Gram's Plymouth, the other the deep treads of Sister Harmony's new Buick. In the kitchen there would be the tell-tale teacups on the counter and the cake crumbs. Chrissa half expected to come home some weekend and find Sister Harmony and the piano player moving into the house.

And then one day, when Thad stayed after school for band practice, she got off the bus and saw that the red flag on the mailbox was sticking straight up. Chrissa reached inside and found an envelope in her own handwriting:

Mr. Nicholas P. Jennings
General Delivery
Watertown, MA

And stamped at the bottom:
UNCLAIMED. RETURN TO SENDER.

Chrissa walked slowly up the drive, as cold inside as she was out. Was this the way it would be, then? Nobody doing a thing till it was too late? What would prevent Gram from giving away not only the woods but her house, as well? First Sister Harmony and her nephew would move in, supposedly to look after Gram, and the next anyone knew, Gram would be out on the street. That, or dead.

She shifted her books to her other arm and unlocked the door. Usually Bess and Shadow were waiting on the other side to greet her, but this time it was someone else: the piano player.

Chrissa froze in the doorway.

He was sitting at the kitchen table, legs crossed, one arm thrown casually over the back of the chair, the long fingers of his other hand drumming lightly on the tabletop. The cats were sitting on the floor beside his chair, grooming themselves, indifferent as to who kept them company.

Chrissa did not move an inch. "How did you get in?" She glanced quickly through the window and saw that he had parked the Buick around behind the house. Obviously he had wanted to take her by surprise, make sure he got inside. In answer, he held up a key and smiled.

"Sister Harmony's had it all along. A lot of people give her their keys, in case of sickness, you know. So Sister can look in on them."

"Well, now that you're in, you'll have to leave. I'm not supposed to have *any*one in here when Gram's not home." Chrissa held the door open, but the man made no move. Didn't even uncross his legs. Just sat at the table bouncing the key up and down in his open palm.

"What do you want?" Chrissa asked.

"Relax, will you? It's time you and I had a little talk." His voice grew more mellow. "Sit down, sit down!"

"I can talk standing up. It's a natural talent," she said dryly.

He laughed. "I've been thinking about you, Chrissa— wondering what makes you tick. And you know what I think?"

"What you think means about as much to me as leftover spinach," she told him.

"What I think is that you haven't been getting a fair

144

shake. Sent out here to your grandma's, not a whole lot to do. A girl without a dad can't have all that much money, and you need money to go places, buy things . . ."

"What is this, a bribe?"

He ignored her. "It's only natural that you should be upset at the idea of your grandmother deeding over her woods to the church. I can understand that. If I was in your shoes, I'd feel the same."

She didn't trust herself to answer.

"I just want you to know that Sister Harmony and I are ready to turn some of that land back over to you. You can keep it, sell it, do whatever you like. Don't want any hard feelings between us."

The only reason Chrissa closed the door was that she was freezing, but she stood with one hand on the knob, ready to flee if necessary.

"It's Gram's land, not yours or mine," she said.

"Face facts, Chrissa. She's deeding a hundred sixty acres to Sister Harmony, whether you like it or not, and I just came by to say that some of it could go to you."

"So what's the catch?"

"Nothing! You don't have to say or do a thing. In fact, that's the whole of it. Just let Elvina do what her conscience tells her. No talking about us behind our backs, no refusing to call your grandma to the phone. Just treat us with simple decency, and ten of those acres are yours."

Chrissa's eyes were on the key again. How long had they had it, and how many times had they been in the house before Chrissa had come, going through Gram's things?

"Get out," she said, opening the door and holding it there.

The piano player seemed surprised.

"What's the matter? Don't you trust me?"

"Like the tail end of a skunk."

"You better think about this, girl. A one-time offer."

"Just go."

He stood up, towering over her there in the kitchen, and reached for his coat. As he did so, the key fell out of his hand onto the floor. In a split second, Chrissa lunged and her fingers closed around it.

He grabbed her wrist, his face within inches of hers.

"You listen to me, darlin'. If anything goes wrong with that property deal, remember this: Sister Harmony always has the last word."

It hadn't happened, then? The deed wasn't signed yet? The knowledge made her hope, and hope gave her courage.

"You take Gram's woods, you'll be the ones who are sorry," she countered.

He gave her wrist an angry shake that made her wince, but her fingers held fast to the key. Staring at her for another moment or two, he let his slow smile spread snakelike over his lips. Then he dropped her hand and left the house, and minutes later Chrissa heard his car drive away.

She did not tell Gram. There was too much at stake here, and time was running out. Gram would say they were being generous, to offer some of that land to Chrissa. That alone might clinch the deal. No, she had another thought about her father: Could there be another Watertown? She'd started with Maine but stopped at Massachusetts.

As soon as she got to school the next day, she stopped by the library to check; got the atlas and moved her finger down the coast, then checked the list of cities for each state.

Rhode Island: none. Connecticut. . . . She stared. *Watertown,* the atlas read. C-3. She was elated and dismayed at the same time. Would she have to check the whole United States? What about the state of New York? Suppose it had a Watertown, too? She checked. It did.

"I've got to make a phone call, Sandy," she said to her friend at lunchtime, hurriedly gulping down the last of her ham sandwich.

"Who? You have a boyfriend back in New York City?"

"A million of them," Chrissa said.

"Yeah? Really, who you calling?"

"Just my dad," Chrissa said offhandedly.

"Oh," said Sandy.

Outside the cafeteria, Chrissa deposited her quarter and dialed information. No, there was no Nick Jennings listed for Watertown, New York. Chrissa put in another quarter and dialed again.

"Watertown, Connecticut," she said, turning slightly, as she saw that Sandy had followed her out. "Do you have a listing for Nicholas Jennings?"

"I'm sorry," came the operator's voice. "I don't find any Nicholas or Nick Jennings."

"Not in?" Sandy asked, as Chrissa hung up.

"Uh-uh."

"He live with your mom?"

"No, they're divorced."

"Welcome to the club," Sandy told her.

Usually attentive in Mr. Bedlow's class, Chrissa let her eyes wander to the window, where new snow was falling. Nature's own ticker-tape parade. She and Thad always lingered on the driveway up to Gram's when it was snowing, so that when they reached the house they were snow-encrusted, and laughed at the vision of each other sixty years into the future, with snow-white brows and hair. Once, Scott had come along, and the three of them had had a snowball fight in Gram's yard, holding the lids of garbage cans for shields. Chrissa felt sometimes as though she were living a double life: Thad and his friends in one, Sister Harmony and the piano player in another. Good and evil.

"I wonder if I could have *every*one's attention," she heard Mr. Bedlow saying, and turned quickly to the front of the room. "I'd like to be out there too, Chrissa, but we have another twenty minutes to go."

At Chrissa's request, Thad stayed with her until she checked out the house that afternoon. His bus had arrived first and he was waiting for her. Then they tramped up the snowy drive together, pointing their feet out with one step, in with the next, the toes and heels coming together so that they formed a diamond pattern all the way up to Gram's.

She told him about the piano player.

"Lucky you got the key back," Thad said.

"I wouldn't sleep nights if I hadn't."

"They could ask your grandmother for another one."

"I doubt it. They'd have to explain what happened to the first, and I don't think they'd want her to know."

Chrissa checked each room and—seeing that all was in order—waved Thad on. Then she took two stamps and envelopes from Gram's desk and sent two more letters, general delivery, to Watertown, Connecticut, and Watertown, New York.

18

Dear Chrissa:

Yes, your letter was a surprise. To tell the truth, I didn't know *how* you were getting along at Gram's, because I so seldom hear from you. Gram writes, of course, but she could be on a sinking ship and still enjoy a sunset—that's how upbeat she is.

My first thought was no, I want you to come home. If we can get along together, I want you here. Then I wonder if the reason you seem to be doing better is because you're at Gram's. If that's the case . . . well, let's think some more about it, okay? You're probably mistaken about her health. I spoke with her a few days ago on the phone. She says her knees are still bothering her, but other than that, she's doing fine. . . .

Mom

Chrissa was partial to Julie, she knew. Each time she went to the Johnsons, she stuck something in her pocket to show the little girl—an old coin purse, magnifying glass, pinecone, blue-jay feather.

She brought paper clips to hook together for a necklace,

149

old tablet paper for outlining hands and feet. Once she brought Gram's prism to catch the slanting rays of winter sun. By hanging it in a window and twirling the string, she made little rainbow butterflies that went dancing about the room, and Julie sat entranced.

Each weekend Gram had been dropping her off a half hour before Mrs. Johnson left for work, so she could help out. The young mother needed it because she was always in the middle of making their breakfast, and seemed distracted when Chrissa spoke to her, blinking her eyes and looking up suddenly as though her mind were a million miles away.

On this morning Johnny was cereal from eyebrow to elbows and gave impatient cries, vigorously swinging one foot when Chrissa slowed at spooning cereal into his mouth.

"Tell you what," Chrissa said to Julie after their mother had left. "I'm going to give Johnny a bath in the sink. You can bathe Susie, too, if you like."

It was a fine idea, because Julie had to remove all the doll's clothes, then get up on a chair and go through the motions of bathing. An activity good for twenty minutes. Sitting in the sink beside Johnny, the large doll was almost as tall, and Julie mimicked Chrissa's motions as she probed at ears and nostrils and wiped under the doll's chin.

Just like her mother, Julie kept up a running patter: "Once Daddy gave me a bath and I got soap in my eyes."

"It hurts, doesn't it?" Chrissa commented, trying to keep Johnny from scraping his back on the faucet. "Do you remember much about your daddy, Julie?"

The little girl nodded, eyes on Susie's arm, which had somehow twisted around behind her back.

"What did he look like? Did he have light hair or dark?"

Julie nodded again.

"Light hair?"

The nod.

"Dark hair?"

The nodding continued.

Chrissa gave her a hug and wrapped Johnny in a towel.

Gram was in a state that evening. Chrissa had never seen her quite like this. She said almost nothing when she came in the house, mouth set determinedly in a straight line. Walked right on by Chrissa to put her bag on the dining room table, then came out in the kitchen to yank a pan from the cabinet below and plunk it on the stove.

"Hard day?" Chrissa asked from across the table, where she was catching up on the week's comics.

For a moment it seemed Gram was not going to answer. Then she muttered, "Work was okay."

Chrissa raised her head and watched the tiny woman. "What happened?"

For a long time Gram did not answer, and Chrissa began to think she wasn't going to. The set of her lips alone told Chrissa that if she were a cursing woman, the oaths would have escaped by now. Then, in words so clipped that they seemed more to be spat from her mouth than spoken: "I've found out some people aren't what they seem."

Chrissa frowned quizzically. "Anyone I know?"

"Sister Harmony, is who."

Chrissa stared. *Finally! Hallelujah!* "What did she do?"

Gram went about answering in her own way. "Trouble with me is, I don't let my ears believe what I can't see with my own eyes, but this time I saw."

151

Hamburger hit the hot skillet with a hiss, and instantly the smell of singed meat filled the kitchen. Gram yanked a spatula off the rack and flopped the meat over, then probed at it with an angry jab.

"Why I trusted her I don't know, but I wasn't the only one who got burned, I'll wager."

Chrissa had no doubt that if she sat long enough without commenting, the whole story would come out, but it might be midnight.

"Ma Jennings, somebody says last week. 'I don't want to pry, but there are folks who believe Sister Harmony's not all she's made out to be.' 'And what's that?' I ask. 'A healer,' the lady tells me. 'Seems like that's for me to decide,' I say, but she keeps at it: 'You give her any money, you've seen the last of it.' And I say, 'I give her any money, I *expect* to see the last of it.'" Gram sighed and shook her head, her mouth tugging down at the corners.

Chrissa began to suspect. "How much did you give her this time, Gram?"

The little woman sank down in a chair and covered her eyes with one hand. "Only the Good Lord kept me from giving her the whole thing, but I had a certificate of deposit come due, and I gave her fifteen hundred."

"Gram!"

"Was there ever a bigger fool?" In rebuke, the old woman slapped her right wrist so hard that the spatula fell to the floor. "Only thing prevented me from writing down the whole ten thousand was the feeling maybe I ought to wait and see what fifteen hundred could do. Told her I'd give her the rest later."

"But what happened?" Chrissa got up and turned the fire off under the frying pan, then sat down again. Her grandmother looked twenty years older right then.

Gram gave a sigh. "Just this morning, in Rochester, I'm coming out of the bank with old Miss Norris on our way to the beauty parlor, and down the block I see Sister Harmony going into a store. Got her nephew with her. I'm all set to holler at her, you know, but she didn't have on her white dress, so I wasn't sure. I wait till I get down to where I saw her go in, and it's a jewelry store. Jeweler's holding up a necklace for her to look at."

If Gram were a child, Chrissa could have picked her up and held her just then. "I suppose there's no law that says a preacher can't buy herself some jewelry," she said gently.

"No law at all," said Gram. "But the fact is, she's telling me that I can't ask God to open his heart to me if I don't open my purse to him. Said that fifteen hundred would keep her on the road preaching and healing for two months, and if I could ever see my way clear to pay for a whole year of the Lord's work, there wasn't one thing too big that the Lord couldn't do for me, all I had to do was ask."

"Gram, do your knees really hurt you that much?"

Gram swallowed and dabbed at her eyes. "Wasn't my knees, Chrissa. Anyway, I got Miss Norris settled in her chair at the beauty parlor, and then I head back down the street to the jewelry store. I wait next door till I see Sister Harmony leave. After a few minutes I go in and tell the jeweler my sister was just in here, and I'm looking to give her a present. Could he please suggest something to go with whatever it was she bought?

"Well, I tell you, he's more than happy, and he shows me another necklace, says it's real close to what she's got, and how about these nice earrings? But all I'm doing is looking

153

at the price tag on that necklace—fourteen hundred and fifty dollars, and I know sure as I got shoes on my feet that it's my check paying for it." Her chin trembled. Trembled so hard Chrissa could see her clamping her teeth together to control it. "I've heard that Sister Harmony's got her a house in Florida you wouldn't believe, and it's folks like us that's bought it for her, but I thought it was all talk. Just jealousy. They ought to lock up women like me, Chrissa. My brain's no better'n butter."

Chrissa had to know. "Gram, tell me: Did you give them the deed to the woods yet? Did that really go through?"

"No, thank Almighty Jesus, I didn't."

Chrissa closed her eyes in relief.

"I could tell you weren't keen on it, and something Mr. Hewlitt said let me know they weren't exactly thrilled at the idea either. I figured I could hold off on that awhile: woods weren't going anywhere. But that only made Sister Harmony and that nephew of hers hungrier still. Kept calling me all the time: When am I going to have a lawyer deed those woods over to them?"

She rested her forehead in her hands and rocked back and forth. "All these months she's wanted more. No matter what I give her, it's not as much as the Lord expects, she tells me. Got me so nervous I couldn't eat. Could hardly sleep some nights, wondering how much I could afford."

"What did you *want* from her so bad, Gram? What was worth all that much?"

Gram sat for a moment, staring down at the table, and finally she said, "The blind to see and the deaf to hear and the lame to walk, and more. That's what she promised me."

"The lame to walk?"

"No. Much more than that." Gram got up slowly and

154

turned the fire on again. "Not anything to do with me at all." She didn't say what.

Gram did not, of course, go to Sunday service that week or the week after. The telephone rang one evening and she answered but, after a terse comment, dropped the phone so abruptly that Chrissa looked up from her book. She didn't ask questions. Didn't need to. Her relief was too complete. Unless Gram had a change of heart, the worst was over. Maybe Sister Harmony had got the drift and would be moving on.

The snow of February became the snow of March—the same deep winter sky spanning the two months. The ice remained on the fish pond, the swing did a rattling, loose-jointed dance in the wind. Once, Chrissa thought she heard the honk of geese returning from their winter nesting grounds. Gram turned the page on the calendar hopefully, as though the very act of turning would bring on spring a little faster.

At school, Chrissa got her essay back from Mr. Bedlow. An A, in red pencil at the top. And in the margin the teacher had written, *Great job, Chrissa. I enjoy having you in my class.* She couldn't seem to stop smiling. Even the return of her letter from Watertown, Connecticut, didn't dampen her spirits.

The first Friday in March, Chrissa and Thad stopped on the driveway to examine a large cocoon on a forsythia bush, then horsed around in the old snow along the drive, making giant footprints of a creature they dubbed the Snowasaurus. They sat together on the swing, moving slowly back and forth, making tracks on the ground beneath.

"So you're going back to the city next summer, huh?" Thad asked after a while.

"That was the plan."

"You sign a contract or anything?"

She laughed. "Not exactly. Maybe Mom would be glad to have me stay another year."

"I know I would," he told her.

Now *that* was a new feeling, Chrissa realized. Knowing that somebody liked her. Maybe more than that.

As slowly as winter was giving way, but as sure as the coming of spring, Chrissa could feel the difference in herself. At times she realized she had not thought of her father for several days. Not even once. There was no urgency in finding him now, of course. And occasionally she wondered what would happen if she never heard from him again. Would she wither away, or would the scar close over, like a tree shorn of a limb?

After Thad left, she went inside and took off her jacket. She had just reached for the Oreo cookies when she heard a car come up the drive. Thinking it was Gram home early, she went on eating, and had turned a page in her biology book propped up before her on the table when there was a rap at the back door. Sister Harmony was peering through the glass.

Before Chrissa could get to her feet to lock it, the door opened and the large woman in the gray coat came inside, filling the kitchen with her presence.

"Gram's not here," Chrissa said, deleting the hello.

"I can see that for myself," Sister Harmony said. Her steel-gray eyes were fixed rigidly on Chrissa. "I didn't come to pay her a visit, my girl. I came to see you."

"Well, save your breath," Chrissa said rudely, "because I'm not buying."

Sister Harmony pulled out a chair and sat down, looking sorrowfully at Chrissa. "What on earth did I ever do to make you hate me so much?"

"Your thug of a nephew, for one," Chrissa replied.

"Chrissa, if he has done anything to frighten you, I do sincerely apologize," the preacher said. ""But what's happened? What's going on with your grandmother?"

Chrissa could only smile. She would not give the preacher the satisfaction of saying why Gram was angry. If she mentioned that necklace, Sister Harmony would twist out some kind of story to make Gram believe she'd bought it for a dying woman or something, and Gram might relent and fork over the rest of her money.

When several moments had elapsed without a response, Sister Harmony said reproachfully. "If you were a daughter of mine, we'd sit face-to-face till we'd talked it out."

Anger coursed up through Chrissa's throat. "Well, lucky for me I'm not," she shot back.

The woman's face was changing again, and the softness disappeared. When she spoke, the softness had seeped out of her voice as well.

"Well, maybe you're not as lucky as you guess." Sister Harmony's eyes narrowed as she studied Chrissa some more. "Think you can just say whatever you want and get away with it. Poison the minds of those around you like a skunk in a well. Maybe you think you've got a charmed life."

"That's the biggest laugh of the year!"

"You turned Elvina against me, didn't you?" Sister Harmony leaned forward and scrutinized Chrissa as though she were studying a bug in a bottle.

"Me?"

157

"Oh, you cooked up some story, I don't doubt. She hasn't come to service the past two Sundays. Won't talk to me on the phone. Why did you turn her so against God?"

"Against God?" Chrissa gasped. "*God?* You and your nephew? Now *that's* the biggest laugh of the year."

Sister Harmony shook her head. "Why, Chrissa, soon as I saw you, I knew you were a bad seed." The sorrowful tone again. "Your mother can't do a thing with you, so she sent you here. Now you're upsetting your grandmother, turning her away from the blessing she was about to receive."

"You've got it wrong there. Any receiving being done, it looks like you're the one who got it."

Sister Harmony stiffened. "You are one sorry sight if I ever saw one." she stood up. "Well, what can I expect, after all? Consider the source, I always say, and I know who *you* sprang from."

"What do you mean?"

There was something disturbing about Sister Harmony's remark. About the changing look in her eyes. "Your *father,* girl! I know about your father."

"What *about* my father?"

The eyes were changing even more, from derision to malice. "He's in Watertown, and nobody's told you, have they?"

"Watertown, New York?"

"Watertown Prison! You've never been upstate? Why, my girl, I can see from your face you had no idea!"

For a few moments Chrissa thought she was paralyzed. She wanted to swallow, but the saliva only collected in the corners of her mouth. Her muscles seemed to have gone dead. Words kept forming at the back of her throat, but her tongue felt so thick it blocked the sound.

Sister Harmony gave a faint smile. "Watertown Prison," she said again, and her eyes seemed almost to glow. "And your grandmother would do anything in the world to turn his life around." Her voice became softer, then; pitying. "I could have done that, too, for I have the healing power that reaches across prison walls. But not now. We're off to Tampa tomorrow, and your dad's got twenty years."

19

Chrissa stood with her hands on her stomach, thinking she was about to be sick. There was a huge hollowness at the back of her throat, the space growing larger and larger as the sound of Sister Harmony's Buick died away.

Everything made sense now, her father's comings and goings, his sudden disappearance for good, Mom and Gram's secretiveness, the last three years of not hearing from him. And then, most ironic of all, the Watertown she'd been seeking was right here in New York State, and it was the last place she'd want her father to be. Could any news be worse than that?

She was still in the kitchen, standing in almost the same position, when Gram came home fifteen minutes later. One look at Chrissa's face and Gram put down her purse.

"You sick?"

"I'm sick." The words sounded hollow.

"What's wrong?"

Anger exploded in Chrissa: "You didn't *tell* me Dad was in prison! You and Mom kept it secret all these years!"

Gram's face blanched and her lips parted. She didn't take her eyes off Chrissa's. "Who's been here?"

"And I had to find it out from *her*! Sister Harmony!"

"God in heaven! . . ."

"Why didn't you *tell* me?" Chrissa was sobbing now, tears of rage.

"Chrissa, honey!" Gram looked at her pleadingly. "Oh, I knew this was all wrong. I wanted to tell you, Chrissie. Really I did. But all Lorraine could think of was what it was like for her at your age. She felt it was just too big a load for a girl to carry." Gram looked sick herself.

"I don't believe any of it!" Chrissa was unstoppable now. "I don't believe he's in prison! How could he be in prison and nobody else know?" She felt she was choking.

"Nobody in Chelsea knew because New York is a big city, and Nick was arrested in Pennsylvania. I told Sister Harmony because . . ." Gram's voice cracked. "Because . . . she said . . . that with the Lord's help, she could change Nick. That her prayers would change him and get him early parole. And I, like the fool that I am, believed her."

Chrissa was still crying. "What did he do?"

"It was a gambling operation strung out over several states. A lot of people were ruined. Two men were killed."

"He *killed* someone?"

"He never confessed to that, but he was convicted of racketeering."

No, it couldn't be!

"If he's in prison, he still could have written to me. Why didn't he write?"

"Lorraine asked him not to. After he went to prison, she just wanted to shut him out of your lives."

Chrissa didn't want to hear it. Wouldn't listen. She turned and ran from the kitchen, rushed upstairs, and threw herself on the bed.

This was what she had waited three and a half years to find out? *Summer's fool and winter's idiot.* All this time Chrissa had fantasized how proud her dad would be to see her going through Gram's woods by herself, petting a dog, climbing a ladder, riding in the back of an open truck. . . . Dad, who had run a first-class con game and possibly even killed someone, admiring *her*? Her and her pitiful little list of accomplishments? Even the way she had stood up to the piano player seemed anemic now.

For the last three and a half years she had missed and admired a criminal who didn't really care about her. *Figure Chrissa's doing okay, you didn't say. You have any photos of her, send me one.* That's all he had to say. Not *Is she well? Is she sad? Is she doing all right at school? Have any friends?* Not for one moment did Chrissa believe he had not written because Mom asked him not to. When had he ever done what Mom wanted before? Well, if he had nothing to say to her, she had plenty to say to him!

It was all for nothing, then, her coming to Gram's? The time she'd spent at the Hewlitts'? Mr. Bedlow's class, Julie and Johnny, the pond, the trees, the woods?

No, a part of her whispered back. *You like yourself; you know you do.* But another voice answered, *Yes, you fool. You've got as much spunk as pudding.*

She didn't come down to dinner. At seven o'clock Chrissa was still lying on her back, eyes on the ceiling. She didn't want to talk with anyone, and didn't see how she could face Thad ever again.

They were quiet at breakfast on Saturday. Chrissa sat opposite Gram at the table, and even the sound of the butter knife scraping toast seemed out of place in the stillness. She

162

ate without tasting, moved without feeling. Prison. Her father Nick, the man who had turned their apartment from cold to warm and warm to cold again, was in prison. The worst kind of father a girl could have.

The sky outside the window had an uncertain look, and the forecast for the weekend was rain or ice or sleet; not even the newspaper was sure.

Gram sucked at her tea, and Chrissa wondered if she'd always made that noise. "I'm ready when you are," Gram said at last, the usual signal that it was time to leave.

Angry still, Chrissa backed away from the table and went upstairs to brush her teeth. She threw her jacket on over her jeans, and then, because the sky looked so cold, pulled her wool cap on her head, took her gloves, and picked up the small bag of wooden spools she'd found in the spare bedroom, so that Julie could play at stringing them.

The wind was sharp as they left the house, catching the storm door and banging it wide open. There was never any heat in the car until a half mile or so before they reached the Guilford driveway. Because it was hard for Gram to back up, she always let Chrissa out at the foot of the winding drive, and Chrissa walked.

This morning Chrissa opened the car door before the Plymouth even came to a stop, then slammed it shut and was relieved when she heard the car pulling away behind her. Whenever she was angry about anything, Gram got it first. It wasn't fair, but who ever said that life was fair?

She had slept very little the night before. Whenever she closed her eyes, she saw her father in prison. Tried to imagine him behind a barred window, in a shapeless uniform. She would shake her head to rid herself of the image, then begin all over again.

She headed up the long driveway, face turned to one side to escape the wind, and was suddenly surprised to see a man standing some distance away looking at her. She slowed only a minute, then kept going as he made no move to come toward her. Her first thought, of course, was the piano player, but then he began walking in the opposite direction. If Sister Harmony's nephew was still around and out to get her, he could do it now. But the man went on.

She turned, walking backward so she could follow him with her eyes. He, too, glanced back, but kept going on down toward the road. He was fairly tall, and wore a heavy parka so that she couldn't make out the shape of his head. When he was out of sight in the heavily wooded lot next to the Guilfords', Chrissa turned forward again. A surveyor, most probably, come to take out these woods. Would there be more, would the woods on the other side of the Guilford house go, and then the woods between the Hewlitts' and Gram's? Maybe all Chrissa had done was rescue the trees from Sister Harmony so the state Roads Commission could have them.

The trees on either side of the curving driveway trembled nervously in the March wind, their branches scraping, limbs bobbing up and down. After she made the turn, Chrissa saw that the giant beech tree up near the house stood guard as always, but it, too, was riled by the wind, and seemed to be shaking its head at the commotion.

When Chrissa got inside, she found the usual mess in the kitchen. Mrs. Johnson had the harried look of a young mother who needed more time than she had to get ready. One bra strap had slid off her shoulder and was visible through the sleeve of her uniform. Orange juice, which had spilled on the table, had already dripped off the edge onto her skirt.

"I'll take over," Chrissa said promptly, and sat down to give Johnny the rest of his applesauce. Julie was lining up Cheerios around the edge of her bowl, then trying to see how many she could stick on the tines of a fork.

Chrissa went about her work distractedly. She knew she was the same person she had been the day before and the day before that, regardless of where her father was or what he had done, and yet . . .? She couldn't wait for Mrs. Johnson to leave—wanted to have a day stretched out before her where she could simply think, with only Julie and Johnny around.

"I've a favor to ask," Mrs. Johnson said, coming back into the kitchen with her coat on. "Tomorrow's my birthday, and the girls at the restaurant are going to take me out after work. I'll be getting back late tomorrow, but if you could stay here until I come . . ."

"Sure," said Chrissa. "No problem." *Just go!* she said to herself.

"Are you mad at me?" came a small voice.

Chrissa realized she had been sitting on one side of the couch for nearly half an hour while Julie watched *Mister Rogers' Neighborhood,* and had not spoken to the child once. Johnny was lying in the playpen on his stomach, sucking his thumb and crooning sleepy noises.

"Of course not. Why do you think that?" Chrissa pulled Julie on to her lap.

"You look mad."

"I do?" Chrissa managed a smile. "Now do I look mad?"

"No." Julie smiled back and snuggled against her.

165

"I guess I was just doing a lot of thinking," Chrissa said, and hugged her tightly. They had to stick together, she and Julie. They were both survivors. Had to go from being hurt to being healed.

Amazing, she thought as Mister Rogers moved and spoke before her eyes and she seemed to see and hear none of it. Amazing that one human being, her father, had controlled for so long not only her happiness but her self-esteem. All this time she'd tried to be the girl she thought *he* wanted her to be. What did *she* want? What kind of person was she really?

It was about eleven o'clock, when Johnny was taking his juice and Julie was making a bridge with her blocks, that Chrissa saw the man again, far back of the house in among the trees. It was only luck she saw him at all, because she could scarcely make out that he was there. If he hadn't moved, she would have missed him. She placed her forehead against the glass and strained to see.

There seemed to be a truck or van of some kind on the service road that paralleled the driveway, almost invisible from where she stood. That was undoubtedly the place the county would pick to put in a road, seeing as how neighbors used it anyway.

Johnny was getting over a cold and was still fussy when Chrissa prepared to put the children down for their naps that afternoon. So she sat in one of the old Guilford rocking chairs in the parlor and rocked him, afraid he would keep Julie awake if she left him upstairs. At four years, Julie napped little enough as it was, and Chrissa always looked forward to that small piece of time for herself.

There was the dull thud of footsteps outside on the steps, then the porch. Chrissa looked up. The doorbell rang. Johnny was almost asleep in her arms, and Chrissa hated to disturb him. Wake him now and he might be up for the next two hours.

She got up very slowly, trying not to jiggle him. The bell rang again. Johnny startled, and Chrissa stood still, waiting until his arms hung heavy. Then she moved slowly out into the hall just as the man in the parka, who had been standing outside the door, moved over to the parlor window, and Chrissa saw him shading his eyes as he peered inside.

Who *was* this person? She couldn't make out the face. Did she dare open the door to him? Could it be one of the surveyors, wanting to use the phone? She started down the hall toward the door just as he turned again and went back down the steps and across the lawn to the trees.

Chrissa watched him go, studying him from the back. *Some*thing about his face—what she had seen of it—seemed familiar, but what? He didn't have the slow gait of the piano player, yet she couldn't be sure.

It wasn't until the man was gone that Chrissa had another thought. Her *father*? Was it possible? Her heart began to thump wildly in spite of herself. It had been impossible to see the shape of his head—the color of his hair, even. But what about the droop of his shoulders? Was that familiar? How could she not remember her own dad?

She leaned against the wall. What if her father had escaped? Maybe he'd got her letter, forwarded from Watertown city to Watertown Prison, about where she was working and wanted to talk to her, away from Gram's, and tell his side of the story—had been watching for her this morning, but hadn't quite recognized her out on the driveway. She had changed a lot over the last three and a half years too. Maybe he *had* got early parole. If you were sentenced to twenty years in prison, what was the earliest you could get out? Her feelings seesawed back and forth. Did she want to see him at all? Maybe *she* didn't care!

If it *is* him, he'll come to the door again, she thought. She would stand just inside it and ask who he was, whom he wanted. Wouldn't open it until she was sure. She'd know when he answered; surely she'd know his voice.

The man did not return, however, and when Mrs. Johnson drove her home that evening, Julie and Johnny in the back seat, Chrissa stared intently through the trees, but it was almost dark. She saw nothing at all. She was on the verge of telling Mrs. Johnson about the man, then stopped. If it *was* her father, she didn't want word getting back to Gram. Having made one mistake, Gram would not make another. She would undoubtedly want to do the right thing, and would call the authorities to say that her son was down here. Well, not until Chrissa had *her* say! Not until she had a chance to tell her father how it had been for *her* all these years!

"You can still sit tomorrow evening? Did you check with your grandmother?" Mrs. Johnson asked as she let her out at Gram's. "I realize you need to get up early the next day for school, but . . ."

"It's okay," said Chrissa. "I'll finish my homework tonight."

It was a quiet meal, not because Chrissa was sulking but because she was thinking. She knew that Gram was watching her from across the table, not knowing what to say, but Chrissa didn't know what to say either. They were polite to each other, and as soon as the dishes were done and put away, Chrissa curled up in a corner of the sofa near the fireplace to read her social-studies text.

168

She was reading about the summer and winter solstices, and about how primitive people became alarmed at the approach of winter, at the earlier and earlier setting of the sun each day, convinced that somehow they had to lure it back; that only human intervention, ritual, and sacrifice could persuade the sun to return. But it was hard to concentrate. And when Gram came in at last, Chrissa put down her book.

"Tell me about my father," she said.

Gram did not look surprised or annoyed or even resigned. She just leaned her head against the back of the rocker. "I guess we both learned something these last few weeks we'd just as soon not know."

"No, I *do* want to know. That's been the trouble: me trying to figure everything out without the slightest clue." Chrissa's voice was more earnest now than angry. "Tell me this," she went on. "When I was emptying out that blue dresser, there was a gun in the bottom drawer. When I looked again, it was gone. Was it Dad's?"

"Yes."

There was a churning in the pit of her stomach. "Then he did kill someone?"

"I don't know. He visited me once and left the gun. I found it after he'd gone. He never asked about it, and I never told him I'd found it. I think he wanted to get rid of it, but why I'd rather not know."

"I don't feel that way, Gram. It's important I know as much as I can so I can understand myself."

"*Yourself!* Chrissie, don't talk like that! What Nick is or did has nothing to do with you! Don't you believe that for one second. *Nobody's* got the right to decide what we think of ourselves. *Nobody.*"

"Then tell me about Dad, and let me decide for myself."

Gram looked at her for a very long time. And then, slowly, with great deliberation, she reached up and lifted the chain from around her neck. She took the key over to the desk and unlocked the bottom drawer. While Chrissa watched, Gram removed a shoebox and came over to sit beside her on the couch.

"Look here. These are things I never wanted you to see, Chrissie." She lifted the lid and handed her the box.

It appeared to be full of papers. A few letters but legal-looking papers as well. News clippings. Silently, curiously, Chrissa lifted a handful off the top.

The earliest date was 1964. A truancy report. A letter from a principal. Notes from teachers. *Nick is a problem both to himself and to his classmates.* . . .

Beneath the handful of notes and letters, an occasional clipping from a local paper: *Disorderly conduct* . . . MAN ARRESTED FOR THEFT. For possession of a weapon. A parole officer's report . . . The slow unraveling of a life. And Gram had kept it all locked away in a bottom drawer as though that could contain the worry and ease the regret.

"Chrissa, from the time Nick was twelve years old, he was a burden to his dad and me. Seemed like if I could make a list of what I wanted in a son, Nicholas would have failed every one of them. How we failed him, I'm not sure, but we must have. I was in my thirties when he came along, and so tickled I didn't know what to do. We spoiled him, I know, and I've paid for it dearly. He got in with the wrong crowd in high school, and from there it seemed like it went from bad to worse. When he married Lorraine, we were so in hopes he would fly right. But . . . well, any fool, I suppose, could have figured out that with him gone so much, he must be up to something. I guess we lived on hope, your mother and I. But to lose Nick . . ."

"And you worry I'll be next."

"I can't *let* you be next! When Lorraine asked if you could stay here for a year, I made up my mind that I was going to do different by you. You don't have to love me, Chrissie. That's too much to ask. Don't even have to like me. All I want to know is I didn't make the same mistakes with you. That I saved one of the two."

Chrissa swallowed. Swallowed again. All three of them—her, Mom, and Gram—frozen inside themselves, each in a different way. "He doesn't even have anything to do with us anymore, and here we are, still letting him run our lives," she said, her eyes moist.

"Oh, Chrissie, isn't it the truth? Sometimes I look at you, honey, at all your hurts, and see a girl waiting for something to come along and change things—like a bush waiting for spring. Sometimes we have to *be* spring, Chrissa; *we* have to be the ones who do the changing."

"Well, now we're doing it," Chrissa told her.

It was the natural order of things that Gram hugged her, that Chrissa hugged back. Chrissa said nothing, but let the tears come.

Finally she blew her nose and asked, "Do the Hewlitts know—about Dad? Does Thad know?" It was important to her.

"The Hewlitts know. I'm sure Thad does, too. That was just a story I made up about Nick not getting along with them. They didn't even know him, but they know where he is. I didn't want to put them on the spot; didn't want you bringing it up."

Chrissa felt angry at first, but then another thought came

171

to her: Thad had known all this time, and it hadn't made any difference. He father just *was*. And *she* was—anything she wanted to be. It seemed a little bit scary—exciting and scary both.

20

Sunday dawned cold and gray. Dampness in the air promised snow or rain by the following morning. Chrissa was both excited and apprehensive that the man would come again, and that he might, by the slightest chance, be her father. She felt revved up inside—ready to face him.

She arrived at Mrs. Johnson's with extra things to amuse the children, knowing she would have them for a longer time. Her eyes scanned the trees as she walked up the drive, but she did not see the man in the parka. Surely he would try again, wouldn't he? Wouldn't just come to the door once and call it quits!

"There's frozen pizza you and Julie can have for dinner. She'll go to bed about eight," Mrs. Johnson said. "Johnny's still not quite over that cold and needs extra sleep. I don't think he'll give you any trouble."

It was easier with Johnny taking longer naps, but Julie's needs just seemed to spread out like cake batter, taking all the extra time there was. Chrissa painted faces on all the wooden spools and Julie put them on a string. They filled the old coin purse with pennies from Mrs. Johnson's change jar, played store, then spread a blanket on the floor of the parlor and had a picnic lunch. When that was over, they lay on their backs and directed the beam of a flashlight in patterns on the ceiling.

It was about three that afternoon, as the children were napping, that the man in the parka came to the door again, and this time, when she heard the knock, Chrissa sprang out of her chair, then stood motionless, heart pounding. Was it he? Would she know his voice?

She made her way cautiously to the front door, the window covered with a thin curtain, and stared out at him. His face was in shadow, however, and she could hardly make him out. It *could* be her father. Definitely could be him. The dark hair—that much she could see. This man had no mustache, but Dad could have shaved it off. Still . . .

"Yes?" she called uncertainly.

The man seemed startled by this voice coming from behind the closed door. He turned toward the sound, and his eyes scanned the curtain.

"Like to speak to the missus," he said.

Again, there was something familiar about him—about his voice, this time—but he definitely was not her father. Of that Chrissa was sure.

"She can't come to the door right now," she responded, her own voice flat with disappointment. She *wouldn't* have a chance to face her father.

Silence from the porch.

"When you think I can talk to her, then?"

It seemed ridiculous to pretend Mrs. Johnson was home when her car was gone, and she wouldn't be able to talk to this man until tomorrow.

"I'm not sure," said Chrissa.

The man turned away impatiently, placing his weight on his other foot, shoulders hunched, hands thrust in the pockets of his parka.

"Could I give her a message?" Chrissa asked.

"No, guess I'll need the missus. We got a problem on the land out here. Like to have her look at it. She's at work, huh? What time you think she'll be back?"

Surveyors. She was right. "It would be best if you came tomorrow morning between eight and eight thirty."

The man in the parka appeared to be thinking. At last he turned his body fully away from her, as though staring out over the yard, and finally went back down the steps without a word.

Chrissa was surprised to find tears welling up in her eyes. She leaned against the door and let them come. Still? Was she missing her father still? Is this what happened when a parent left, no matter what he had done? Like primitive people imploring the sun to return, was she destined to go on forever plotting and scheming to lure him back? *Why,* when so many of her memories were painful ones? His impatience with her, the looks of disgust, the tone of his voice. Why would she miss a father like that? Because he was the only father she had?

No, it was something else, and Chrissa saw it more clearly than ever before. Perhaps it wasn't her own father she was missing as much as the dad she wanted him to be.

"Chrissa" came a small voice from the top of the stairs. "Can I get up now?"

"You just barely lay down, Julie!"

"Uh-*uh*! I've slept a long, long, long time."

"Lie down and close your eyes."

"They won't *stay* closed! I tried!"

Chrissa sighed. "Okay, get your shoes and come on down." The little girl danced happily back down the hall.

The rain began about nine that evening. It had been a full evening of making paper cutouts, playing hide-the-thimble, taking a warm bath, and reading stories. Johnny had slept most of the afternoon, and Chrissa had had him up for only a few hours when he seemed eager for his bed once again. Probably as close to a trouble-free baby as you could get, Chrissa decided. Julie, however, was never ready for bed. Chrissa was in and out of her room four times, reciting various bedtime chants before Julie consented to turning out the light for good.

Outside, the wind rose and rain slashed at the windows, an icy, spitting sound. It would die down for a time, then come again, a little stronger. The phone rang at ten.

"Chrissa" came Mrs. Johnson's voice. "I should have started out earlier, but we were having such a good time, we didn't realize how late it was. Now there's sleet out there and I've never been very good at night driving. Polly wants me to stay over. Could you possibly manage? I'll set out first thing tomorrow and will be there in time to drive you to school."

"I suppose I can," Chrissa said reluctantly. "I'll need to stop by Gram's in the morning for a few things."

"Of course. Wear anything of mine you need. I'll try to be there by seven thirty."

Chrissa hung up and faced the prospect of staying there all night. She dialed Gram's number.

"I don't blame her," Gram said when she'd heard. "Mrs. Hewlitt just had an accident on the road out here. Nobody hurt, but their pickup's got a big dent in it. Surely not the kind of weather I'd be out in. Thad called, asking about you."

Strange that mere words could make her so warm, Chrissa was thinking.

The phone rang immediately afterward. Thad.

"Want me to come over and sleep on the porch? Guard the house?" he asked.

She laughed. "Like a watchdog, you mean?"

"Something like that."

"If I hear any noises, I'll call you in the middle of the night. Okay?"

The house began to get cold around eleven, and Chrissa decided that the thermostat had probably switched to a night time setting. There was a fireplace and a little wood stacked beside it, but Chrissa knew she would be going to bed soon, so it hardly seemed worth either turning up the heat or lighting the fire. Rummaging about in Mrs. Johnson's closet, she found an old shirt to sleep in and quickly crawled under the comforter on the bed.

It had taken her about six months to get used to the noises in and around Gram's, but here there was a whole new set—buzzing clock, a loud humming noise from the refrigerator downstairs, a shutter banging . . .

She got up once to check on Julie and Johnny, then made the rounds one more time to make sure all the doors were locked, glad to get back under the covers again. The warmth of the bed relaxed her, and her legs began to feel heavy, then her arms, until they seemed to sink into the mattress and become weightless. She dreamed that the man in the parka came back again, and this time, when he took the jacket off, she saw that it was her father after all.

177

Sometime in the night, she didn't know when, she was half-awakened by a cracking sound. Reluctant to let go of her dreams or leave the warmth of the bed, she slumbered on. A few minutes later, however, the noise came again, only this time from another direction—a sharp cracking sound, like a rifle, and then—four or five seconds later— *whoom!* A thud, and a noise like shattering glass.

Chrissa's eyes came open and she stared up at the ceiling, heart pounding painfully. Someone was breaking in!

The piano player? Had he followed her here? Had they not left for Tampa after all?

She threw off the comforter, her chest aching in fright. Swinging her legs over the edge of the mattress, she sat up. The room was freezing. Should she get the children and lock them all in one of the bedrooms?

Another crash, a thud, and the shattering, tinkly sound again. Farther away this time. Once again, silence. What in the world . . . ?

Fear gave way to puzzlement. Somehow the sounds did not seem connected with the house at all. She stood in the middle of the floor, comforter draped around her shoulders, and made her way over to the wall, groping for the light switch. She found it and flicked it, but nothing happened.

Fear again. No lights. No electricity. Opening the door, she saw only the darkness of the hallway, and moved toward the stairs, one hand out in front of her, blanket dragging the floor. She listened again, testing. Strained to hear the slightest sound.

Chrissa groped her way downstairs, trying to remember where she had put the flashlight. She found it at last on top of the refrigerator and, shining a path ahead of her, walked

178

toward the front door. Then she stopped, for even in the darkness she could see the terrifying shape of something huge outside on the porch. Men? Several men now, all carrying rifles? Yet the silence . . .

When the shapes did not appear to be moving, she crept quietly to the window and shone the light through the glass. Then she sucked in her breath, for there, just beyond, lay a huge limb from the beech tree, making a jungle of the porch.

This time Chrissa went to the door and opened it, shining the light all around.

Ice. Ice covering the whole of the limb, every branch, each twig, entombed in a thick glass coating.

She moved the beam of the flashlight slowly over the yard beyond. It was no yard she recognized, but a jungle of branches. Even as she stood there in her bare feet, a great cracking, splitting sound came from the left of the house, then the reverberating thud as a limb hit the ground, followed by the tinkle of shattering ice, not glass.

Ice storm.

She had never seen such a thing in New York City, never imagined it could be so destructive. She knew immediately that the power lines were down, and realized that she should not be standing out here with the door open behind her.

Quickly she went back inside and shut the door, locking it once again, and shone the flashlight on the clock. Three seventeen. She remembered the battery-operated clock in the kitchen and shone the light there. Five fifty-six.

She would sleep no more, and went upstairs to wash and dress. The water was only tepid. She put on her clothes hurriedly, goose bumps on her arms. Maybe she could get the fireplace going so Mrs. Johnson wouldn't have to come home to a totally cold house.

Chrissa went downstairs. First find the flue. It was different from Gram's, but enough alike that she finally got it open. She put all the wood from the basket onto the grate, arranged the logs the way she had seen Gram do back at her place, crumpled up an old newspaper to stick beneath them, then lit it.

Her first effort burned for a minute or two, then went out. She took the poker and made spaces between the logs, then lit more papers. This time the twigs caught, and soon the fire was snapping smartly, one flame catching hold of another, then another, until they were whirling together and the fireplace was filled with their dance. As long as Chrissa was within three feet of it, she felt warmed. Farther than that, her skin was chilled.

With the fire lit and the screen in place, she went from window to window, staring in astonishment across the half-lit landscape as the sky gradually brightened. As far as she could see, there was nothing but an icy tangle of branches.

Johnny was awake, giving little bleats from upstairs, so Chrissa changed him, wrapped him in a blanket, and carried him to the front door to survey the porch again.

"Ice!" she said, pointing. "Ice." He stared at her finger, then at her, and she laughed.

By the time it was full light, Julie was up and standing at the top of the stairs, doll in her arms, her face full of puzzlement and sleep. She dug her fist into one eye, looking cross, then rubbed her right foot against the shin of her other leg.

"Julie, come look!" Chrissa told her.

Jerkily the little girl came down the steps one at a time,

180

trying not to trip over her gown. She padded toward Chrissa and stared out the front window, blinking.

"There was an ice storm!" Chrissa explained. "The rain turned to ice in the night, and it's so thick and heavy that tree limbs are breaking off."

"Where's Mommy?" Julie's voice sounded anxious.

"She had to stay in Rochester overnight. It was just too stormy to drive. She said she'd be here this morning, but with all this ice, I don't know. . . ." Chrissa went back into the kitchen to turn on the TV, then remembered. She took milk from the refrigerator for Johnny.

"Don't worry," she said to Julie. "I'll stay right here until Mommy comes. Let's eat our cereal by the fireplace." Chrissa set to work putting things on a tray.

As they passed the dining room window, she could not help staring out at the lacy world beyond. The branches of every tree drooped downward, bent unnaturally beneath the weight. It was both awful and beautiful, and Chrissa felt as much a part of the ice as she did the rain. It just *was*.

The ice storm did not seem beautiful at all to Julie. Each of Chrissa's remarks was followed by a question: "How will Mommy get here?" "When will the lights come on?" "When can we watch TV?"

The phone rang at a quarter of seven. Thank goodness there was still the phone.

"Chrissie, you okay?" came Gram's voice. "Lord! The look of things here! I've lost a limb off my sycamore."

"I know. We've got the beech tree all over the front porch," Chrissa told her.

"Mr. Hewlitt was out trying to clear the road, so he stopped up here to see if I was all right. He says the police aren't letting cars through—branches and wires down all over the place. I'm surprised our phone wires aren't down too. Schools are closed, of course, so you might just as well sit tight. If Mrs. Johnson's started out already, she'll not get very far."

"I've got a fire going in the fireplace. I think we're okay," Chrissa told her.

"Call me if you need to," said Gram.

Chrissa had scarcely hung up when the phone rang again.

"I feel so awful!" Mrs. Johnson said. "I should have come home last night regardless. Now they're telling us not to go out until they get the power lines up."

"The schools are closed," Chrissa told her. "There's nowhere I have to go."

When it rang again, it was Thad. "Hey, kid, how you doing?"

"I hear it's crazy out there," Chrissa said.

"Pretty awesome. Of course, the schools are closed, so it's not all—"

The line went dead. Chrissa sighed and felt real regret that she was stuck here when she could have been out tramping around with Thad and Scott, being part of the general excitement. When she caught Julie looking at her apprehensively, however, she said cheerfully, "Guess what? We're going to make a cave." They put a blanket over a small table in one corner and crawled under.

Later, when Johnny went down for his morning nap, Chrissa realized they needed more wood. She rummaged through Mrs. Johnson's closet until she found a cardigan, and put it over her sweat suit. Then she and Julie sorted through the pile of clothes in the child's room for long pants, shirt, and sweater. Double socks inside her shoes.

Whatever Julie was allergic to outside was frozen now, of that Chrissa was sure. They had to have heat, and she wouldn't leave a lively four-year-old alone in the house.

"I'll give you a sack, and I want you to put all the little sticks in it you can find. I'll bring in the big stuff," Chrissa told her. "Can you do that for me?"

Julie nodded.

They went out the back door dressed like hockey players. The woodpile was at the end of the yard, and Chrissa had brought a hammer to hack at the ice encrusted on top. She pointed out the path they should take to avoid falling limbs, keeping to the grass for more traction. They made a trip together, Julie following Chrissa's footsteps. Back and forth, back and forth, each going at her own speed now, calling out "Toot toot" whenever they passed.

Meanwhile, despite the devastation, the cold air was invigorating, the scene spectacular. Small bushes were bent double, their tips touching the ground, fancy weblike designs of crystal. As the sun began to climb, the ice shone like jewels, the yard a palace of shimmering diamonds. Every so often Chrissa simply stopped and gaped as another limb somewhere came thudding to the ground, followed by the sound of shattering crystals.

Julie began to complain of the cold. A few more trips, Chrissa knew, and she'd do no more. She placed her own armload of logs at the back door and had just turned again when she saw something move to the right of the woodpile.

The man. He was coming around the pile from behind. Chrissa took a step forward, but before she could even cry out, the man in the parka lunged toward the small girl, who was already heading back with her paper sack, and grabbed

183

her from behind, lifting her up in his arms. Before she could make more than a startled shriek, he had his hand over her mouth and was disappearing back into the trees.

21

A terror Chrissa had never known.

"Julie!"

She ran a few steps forward. The man whirled about. "Get back!" he said brusquely. It was then she saw the knife.

Chrissa stood immobile as he disappeared among the branches, the ice crackling with every step he took. She could not even blink. She was rigid with fear. A few minutes later she heard the sliding slam of a van door.

Call the police!

She turned and ran headlong into the house, bolting the door behind her, then remembered the phone lines were down. She rushed to a window, her breath coming out in noisy gasps. She could barely make out the side of the van far back on the old service road. It must have been there all night, and certainly could not get out again so easily. As soon as she heard the motor start, however, she would run outside, get the license number, and run to a neighbor's. . . . No, she would have to take Johnny.

Get Johnny up and run to a neighbor's?

Even without the downed trees and wires, it would take

fifteen minutes to reach someone—down the driveway and then around. No, much longer than that. But it would be difficult for the van as well, and maybe . . .

There was no sound of the van starting up. The thought of what might be happening to Julie! For a moment Chrissa's legs seemed on the verge of collapse. He was no surveyor. He must have been camped there since yesterday, waiting. . . . But why, if he was a kidnapper, hadn't he simply broken in during the night? He must know that Chrissa was alone.

"Oh, my god," she said again and again, more a mantra than a prayer.

And then, through the kitchen window, she saw the man coming alone through the icy jungle. Coming for her!

She whirled around, desperately looking for a place to hide, and rushed into the living room. Should she try to take Johnny and escape?

Grabbing the poker, then racing back to the kitchen, she peered at him through the window of the door as he trudged through the yard, the large knife in his hand. She breathed through her mouth, trying to quiet her heart.

All the possibilities ran through her mind: *Murderer. Psychopath. Child molester.* Was he after ransom?

Bam! Bam! Bam! The back door seemed to shudder with the force of his blows.

He was crazy! He had to be. After kidnapping Julie, he thought Chrissa would answer the door? Something told her to talk to him. She moved toward the curtained window.

"What do you want?" she called.

"I want the boy. Bring me Johnny."

He knew his name!

"Who are you?"

"Their father, and I want my children. You give me Johnny, I won't make any trouble for you."

The father?

"The father's dead. Mrs. Johnson's a widow!"

"Mrs. who, now?"

"Johnson."

He gave a sharp laugh. "It's Mrs. Clyde Early, is who she is."

Mrs. Clyde Early! Where had she heard that name?

"I tracked her as far as Rochester, and I've been driving out here couple times a month from Ohio looking for her. Found out last week where she was, and decided to pay her a visit. A little birthday surprise."

The man in the van! The Ohio license plate!

"I—I didn't know." It was all Chrissa could manage.

"Eight months ago, two days before my birthday, she took off with Julie and Johnny. I'm just returning the favor. A man's got a right to his children. I wanted her to be here when I took the kids, see how *she* likes it, but it doesn't look like that's about to happen." He leaned closer to the glass. "She didn't come home at all last night, did she? Figures."

Chrissa felt as though all the breath had been squeezed from her.

"J-Julie thinks you're dead!"

"That's what she's been told. What everybody's been told, I hear."

Chrissa felt surprise, then relief, sweep over her. If he was the father, he certainly wasn't going to hurt them. So *this* was the story—his wife was hiding from him. *Secrets! These stupid secrets!*

187

What did she really know about Mrs. Johnson—Mrs. Early—anyway? Maybe she hadn't even spent the night in Rochester with girlfriends! She could have been seeing another man on the side. All this time the father had been looking for his children. Missing his little girl. Missing Johnny. But still, Chrissa didn't unlock the door.

Why was Mrs. Johnson hiding? And what loving father would frighten his child that way and carry her off?

"Look," she called finally. "I don't know anything about you or what's happened between you and your wife, but I've got to take care of the children until their mother gets back. Then you can discuss it with her."

"I don't have nothing to say to her. I want my boy."

"If you hurt Julie . . ."

"I'm not going to hurt her. She's my own flesh and blood. But I'll do what I have to do to get my son. You go get him, hand him over to me, and I won't hurt you."

Chrissa's heart raced. Why *wouldn't* a father be upset? They were his children as much as Mrs. Early's. If only she could talk it over with Gram.

She moved toward the phone and lifted the receiver to see if there was any connection yet. Still nothing.

Perhaps she didn't have to do anything. If he was their father, Julie was safe. Frightened, maybe, but safe for the time being. And he wouldn't leave without Johnny, obviously, so he wasn't going anywhere.

He was pounding on the door again. "You open the door or I'm coming in. I'll break the glass."

She blinked. Father or no father, should she trust him one minute?

"You can break a window if you want, but you try to get in here, I'll use the poker. And I'm strong," she added.

188

He cursed, which only strengthened her resolve.

"I'm going to get you out of there, and I don't have to come in to do it," he yelled. "I'll set fire to the house, and you've got no phone. I can see the line down out here."

"The smoke will bring the fire department," she said, calling his bluff.

He was staring right into the curtain now, and even though Chrissa couldn't see his eyes, she felt he could see hers. "I want my *boy*. Bring me my *boy*!" His voice was rising.

She thought again of the way he had grabbed Julie. The way he had brandished the knife. If he wasn't crazy, he was desperate, and if people were desperate enough, they acted half crazy.

"Listen," she said, trying to steady her own voice. "What will you do with them? How do I know they'll be safe?"

"They're with me, they're safe," he said. "A man don't hurt his own children without reason."

Without reason? Would she even *consider* turning Johnny over to this man?

"You bring me my son or I'll smoke you out. I'm not waiting out here all day."

"All right." Her mind raced on ahead of her, spinning out a story. "If you're their father, you can have them. Johnny's sleeping now, but he's been very sick. Both the children have been sick, and Julie needs her medicine."

"I'll take care of that," the man said. "You give it to me, I'll see she takes it."

Could she possibly carry this out? Chrissa began to doubt it. *Show a little spunk, Chrissa. . . .*

"I'm not letting Julie go until she's had her medicine. She's diabetic, you know."

189

"What?"

"You didn't know that? You didn't know she has to have insulin?"

"When did they find that out?"

"A month ago. She has to have injections. I'll get Johnny ready, but I won't give him to you unless you bring Julie back so I can give her an injection. I'll show you how to do it."

"You trying to trick me, girl?"

"No. I'll give you Johnny while I get Julie ready. You'd better take some of the children's clothes with you, too. And some bottles for Johnny."

"Now you're talking sense."

"Give me about fifteen minutes, then bring Julie back. I'll try to dress the baby without waking him."

The man turned again and picked his way through the icy branches in the backyard.

In a frenzy, hands cold with tension, Chrissa spun around, her mouth dry. Her breathing was noisy. She grabbed Julie's doll, then raced upstairs and dressed it quickly in a pair of Johnny's overalls, his small sneakers on its feet, wrapping the laces around the ankles twice to keep them on. If Mrs. Johnson—Mrs. Early—had left her husband nine months ago, Johnny would have been only a month old at the time. That's the way the father would remember him.

Oh, please, please let this work! . . .

She yanked a blanket off Julie's bed and hurried back down with the doll. The body seemed heavy enough, but the arms and legs were too light. Desperately she looked around the kitchen, then jerked the change jar from the counter and dumped some coins on the table. Grabbing fistfuls of pennies, she stuffed some in the doll's stockings, the underpants, the cuffs in the knit shirt—anywhere at all she could put coins where they wouldn't fall out or rattle.

She tried again, picking up the doll. Perhaps. She had to risk it.

Chrissa could hear the man's footsteps coming back across the icy yard. She pulled a wool cap of Johnny's down low over the doll's head, then wrapped the doll carefully in a blanket, around and around, careful to keep the head and face covered.

Johnny, don't wake up! she prayed, glancing toward the floor above. *Please don't wake up and cry!*

Her pulse throbbed in her ears as she worked. Julie was coming up the back steps now, her hand in the hand of the man in the parka.

Chrissa watched her come. The little girl's face was drawn, streaked with tears. She was choking back sobs, her head bobbing with each breath.

"You hush up!" The man said roughly, jerking her hand hard, jarring her whole body. "I told you now, *hush up!*"

Chrissa had the doll in her arms. As the man came to the back door, she opened it, one finger to her lips.

"Johnny's sound asleep," she cautioned. "Hold him as gently as you can, and don't let the wind hit his face. He was up all night with the croup."

The man studied her; Chrissa studied the man—the deep-set eyes. He had that somewhat glassy, unfocused look of a man at odds with the world.

"I seen you before," he said. "You're the girl out on the highway. Said you didn't know Mrs. Early."

Chrissa whispered back. "I didn't know her real name."

Satisfied, the man held out his arms. "Give me my boy."

Chrissa placed the doll in them, and felt Julie sliding in behind her through the doorway. The man started to come in too, but Chrissa nudged him out again. "Shhh," she whispered. "Go lay him down and come back for Julie. She'll chatter and wake him before you can leave."

The man hesitated.

"Please let him sleep. He's been really sick," Chrissa said.

The man started to walk away, his arms stiffly out before him, holding the doll. Then he turned. "Don't you trick me now," he said again.

Chrissa softly closed the door and, as soon as he was off the steps, quietly latched the lock.

"H-he . . . he's not dead. . . ." Julie sobbed. There was a large red handprint on her face.

Chrissa threw on her coat. "*Listen* to me, Julie! We've got to get Johnny and run. And you've got to be very, *very* quiet."

She tore upstairs and lifted a sleeping Johnny. He woke, then whimpered and twisted around in her arms, wanting his bed. Taking one of his blankets with her, Chrissa wrapped it around him, then fled back down through the hall, pulling Julie toward the front door.

"Hang on to me," she said.

Julie, her eyes wide and frightened, obeyed.

They slipped out, closing the door noiselessly behind them. Sleepy-eyed and dumbfounded, the baby sucked in his breath as the wind hit his face. Chrissa led them around the tangle of branches on the porch, looking for wires, stepping gingerly until they were clear of the house. Then they ran.

There was a cracking sound as another limb fell, ripped

from a tree. Several more had fallen since she'd looked over the yard that morning. All around them the icy branches hung white-encrusted and heavy. Right before her eyes, a monstrous limb gave way. *Kaboom!* She could feel the thud in her feet.

Then there was another sound. The rolling slam of a van door. And suddenly the air was filled with a hoarse bellow, then curses.

"I'll get you, girl! I'll kill you!"

Heavy crunching footsteps back behind the house, each like an explosion in Chrissa's ears. Julie began to cry, then screamed in fright. Now the man knew they were out here. Chrissa could not count on his searching the house first.

Oh, god.

Scrambling, climbing, pulling Julie behind her, her breath coming out in short, white puffs, Chrissa made it over the fallen limb. The man roared again, and Chrissa glanced over her shoulder to see him coming around the side of the house.

She scooped up Julie in her other arm. Holding each child around the waist like bags of laundry, she ran. There was still another tree down just ahead. She did not know her arms could do this. Never knew they had the strength. Would never have believed she had the courage.

More curses—footsteps. Running footsteps now.

Crack! The splitting sound of ripping bark. They shouldn't be out here, trees all around. *Whomp!* A cry. Was it possible? She listened, straining to hear. The man had not been hit, because very shortly he was bellowing again, but Chrissa knew he had been slowed.

She ran on, around the bend in the driveway, the four-year-old under one arm, the baby in the other. Far ahead she could see linemen out on the road. See their yellow hard hats, their Levi jackets. She would not look back again. That world was behind her now.

She yelled, sure that she made no sound, hearing nothing but the wind, the pounding of her heart, and, somewhere behind, the angry footsteps once again of Mr. Early. Yet the linemen turned her way.

Now they were moving forward. Coming toward her, faces concerned, hands outstretched.

"Hey now, miss, you're all right!" an older man called, puzzled.

She was surrounded at last by strong arms. Surrounded by trees. Surrounded by sky.

22

Chrissa sat on the couch in Gram's living room beside Thad. He had one arm around her, and Gram didn't say a thing. The late-afternoon sun left a path of light on the rug beside the investigating officer's foot. Bess and Shadow both lay down in it to take what comfort they could.

"You've been very helpful, Chrissa," the policeman said. "I only hope that if my own daughter ever finds herself in a situation like that, she handles it as well as you did."

"Would he have hurt his children?" Chrissa asked.

"That's a hard call to make." The officer closed his notebook. "He was incoherent after they subdued him, the linemen told us, and he's undergoing observation. We've talked to Mrs. Early, and she said her husband had been violent before, mostly toward her, but had begun roughing up the children. That's when she left. Sometimes, with a man like that, all it takes to set him off is a baby crying. You never know."

Chrissa thought of the two small children asleep on her bed upstairs, waiting for their mother to get here. Thought of Julie meeting face-to-face the father she thought was dead.

"Will Julie be all right? She was so frightened," Chrissa said.

The officer reached for his coat and stood up. "I think so. But it would have been a lot better if she'd been told the truth—'Daddy's not well,' that sort of thing. Kids can accept almost anything if you level with them."

Gram walked him out through the kitchen to the back door, and Thad leaned over and nuzzled Chrissa's cheek. "You okay?" he whispered.

"Still shaking inside."

"So am I, when I think about you." He gave her shoulder a hug.

Dear Chrissa:

Ever since your phone call the other night, I have been going over and over the last three and a half years in my mind. More than that, the last fifteen. I can't really blame anyone else for the choices I made. Marrying Nick seemed like a good idea at the time, and we did have some good days together, more than a few.

I think I realized right from the start that Nick meant trouble, but I was insecure enough to need his attention. At the same time, he always seemed to be in a scrape of some sort. As it turned out, I didn't know the half of it.

I guess I could say that the last fifteen years of my life were wasted, if it wasn't for you. But it doesn't mean that the next fifteen have to be wasted, too.

It was a mistake not to tell you about your dad. I thought of myself as a teenager and how ashamed I was of mine. I hope you can forgive all my failings as a mother and remember the ways I succeeded.

Right now, my biggest wish is for you to be happy,

196

and if things are working out for you at Gram's and you want to stay longer, you can. I'd like to come visit you, though, this spring. Could I?

Much love,
Mom

Dear Mom:

Yes, I forgive you, and hope you'll forgive my silences, too. Sometime I'll tell you all that has been going through my head, but I don't want to do it in a letter. I'd like for you to visit this spring. I'd like you to meet Thad, too, and go for a walk in our woods. That would be a good place to start.

Love you.
Chrissa

On Saturday, Chrissa sat beside Gram in the Plymouth and helped her guide the car backward down the drive. There were still too many limbs down around the house for her to turn around there. Mrs. Johnson—no, Mrs. Early—was already moving into an apartment in Rochester with her children to make a new beginning. It was a new beginning for Chrissa, too.

"Watch my mailbox," said Gram. "Don't let me hit it."

"You're okay," Chrissa told her.

The car came to a stop in the middle of the highway, then began moving forward, Gram sitting high at the wheel. It was a three-hour drive to Watertown, by Gram's estimate, and they'd have lunch on the way. Chrissa wore her jacket from last year, the one with the fake fur around the hood. She felt snug and protected inside its fleecy warmth.

"He knows we're coming, doesn't he?" she asked.

"Yes, he knows."

"What did he say?"

"At first I don't think he was too crazy about the idea. Then he said he'd like to see you."

"He actually said that?"

"Well, he said, 'If she wants to come, it's okay with me.'"

It was not what Chrissa had hoped he might say, but she wanted to see him nonetheless. Wanted to look him straight in the eyes and let him know the kind of person she had become: her own kind of person. If he ever found out what she had done for Julie and Johnny, it would be from someone else. That belonged to her alone. She had not done it for her father—was not bringing it to him like a completed assignment. She no longer needed his grades. Chrissa wasn't even sure she needed to tell him off; she'd see when she got there. What she was feeling for her father now was neither fear nor anger so much as pity.

There were still fallen branches along the highway as far as the eye could see. Each time they passed a crossroad, Chrissa saw long rows of bundled sticks and branches at curbside, waiting for pickup.

She rolled down her window to help defrost the windshield. The air felt fresh and cold and crisp—new breath for the ravaged landscape. On either side of the highway, sunlight shone on the strange white splits in the trees where, only a week before, branches had been. Scars, waiting to heal.

EPILOGUE

During the great ice storm of 1991, in the absence of city lights, people noticed how bright the night sky was over Rochester. "Sometimes," a woman said, "it takes an episode like this to make you see the stars."